J
636.7   Cohen, Susan
CO
         What kind of dog is
         that?

$12.95

DATE			
MR 1 '90	MAY 30 '97	JL 14 '22	
MR 16 '90	AUG 22 '97		
MY 4 '90	MAY 07		
MR 23 '91	OCT 14		
03 '94	03		
APR 06 '95	MY 24 '99		
	AP 18 00		
	AG 15 00		
MAY 18 '95	JY 26 01		
DE 18 '95	OC 21 02		
JL 8 9 96	OC 19 '05		
OCT 02 96	OC 04 '06		
APR 28 '97	AG 27 10		

© THE BAKER & TAYLOR CO.

What Kind of Dog Is That?

What Kind of Dog Is That?

Rare & Unusual Breeds of Dogs

Susan and Daniel Cohen

*Illustrated with
photographs*

Cobblehill Books
Dutton   New York

Library of Congress Cataloging-in-Publication Data
Cohen, Susan, date
    What kind of dog is that? : rare and unusual breeds of dogs / Susan
    and Daniel Cohen.
        p.   cm.
    Bibliography: p.
    Includes index.
Summary: Discusses the history, physical characteristics, and behavior
of twenty-five unusual dog breeds including the Fila Brasileiro, the
Peruvian Inca Orchid, the Jack Russell Terrier, and the Chinese Crested.
        ISBN 0-525-65011-3
        1. Dog breeds—Juvenile literature.   [1. Dog breeds.]   I. Cohen,
Daniel.   II. Title.
SF426.5.C635   1989
636.7′1—dc20   89-34462   CIP   AC

Published in the United States by E.P. Dutton,
a division of Penguin Books USA Inc.
Published simultaneously in Canada by
Fitzhenry & Whiteside Limited, Toronto
Designed by Charlotte Staub
Printed in the U.S.A.
First Edition   10 9 8 7 6 5 4 3 2 1

*To Fergie,
our Clumber Spaniel,
recognized but still unusual*

Contents

What Kind of Dog Is That?

Chinese Cresteds and Xolos, some of the country's rarest dogs.

Introduction
What Is a Rare Dog?

Some years ago the *New York Times* ran a story about a young woman who owned a little hairless dog called the Xoloitzcuintli (pronounced zow-low-eats-queen-tlee). That's the breed of dog that was once popularly called the Mexican Hairless. It's called the Xolo (zo-low) for short. She used to walk the dog in Central Park. The Xolo, or any dog without hair, is bound to attract lots of attention. There were not very many of them in the United States. So every time the young woman took her dog out for a walk she was constantly being stopped by people asking her what kind of dog she had. It was often an hour or more before she could get back to her apartment. Finally, she had a little pamphlet printed up describing the breed. She would just hand it to anyone who asked about the dog.

The Xolo is truly a rare breed. You have probably never seen one. You may never have even seen a picture of one. We're going to tell you all about the Xolo in this book.

We're also going to tell you about the Shar-Pei. Those are the dogs that have the unbelievably lovable and extremely wrinkled puppies. It's possible you have never actually seen a Shar-Pei, though they are not that uncommon anymore. You have certainly seen pictures of them. Pictures of Shar-Peis appear in advertising, on calendars, and on greeting cards. There are thousands of these dogs in the United States. But they are still considered rare. So are most of the Coonhounds, though there are lots of them in rural areas, particularly in the American South. Other dogs like the Shiba are common in their native land, in this case Japan, though still not well known in the United States.

Breeds like the Shar-Pei and the Coonhound and the Shiba are all considered rare because they are not breeds recognized by the American Kennel Club—the AKC.

The AKC is the organization that oversees all purebred dogs in the United States. When people talk about a dog being "pedigreed" or having its "papers" they usually mean that it is registered with the AKC. In most dog shows you will see only breeds recognized by the AKC. If you pick up a book on different breeds of dogs in America, chances are that only those dogs recognized by the AKC will be covered.

There are lots of reasons why a particular breed may not be recognized by the AKC. Usually it is because there are not enough representatives of the breed in this country, or they have not been in the United States long enough. Some rare dog owners just don't want their breeds recognized by the AKC, because the AKC has a lot of rules and restrictions.

All the rare breeds have their own organizations. There are special shows for rare breeds only. Many breeds are working toward recognition by the AKC. They are in what is called the Miscellaneous Class of the AKC. But they still are not eligible to be shown in regular shows. And they still won't be found in most dog books.

However, it seems that rare breeds are more popular today than they have ever been before. Why do people like rare breeds? Some just like to be different, own a dog that very few other people own. Others like to get in first and help to establish a new breed in the United States. For some people a particular dog expresses their national heritage. The Polish Sheepdog, for example, is most popular among Polish-Americans. Some people just see a particular breed and fall in love with it, no matter how odd other people think it is.

Owning rare breeds can be demanding. The dogs are often hard to get. Sometimes they must be brought in from another country. They can be very, very expensive. And since the breed is not well known, the dog may have health or temperament problems that the owner did not know about or expect.

Rare breed ownership certainly isn't for everyone. But for some people it's the most rewarding kind of dog ownership in the world.

So get ready to meet some of the rare and unusual dogs that you won't read about in most other dog books. And if you happen to see somebody walking a Peruvian Inca Orchid or a Catahoula Leopard Dog, you won't have to ask them, "What kind of dog is that?" because you will already know.

3

Alp Arslan Bey, an Akbash Dog, takes a look at a litter of his puppies.

1. The Akbash Dog

The Akbash Dog, or something very like it, has been guarding the flocks and herds of Turkish shepherds for hundreds, perhaps thousands, of years.

In Turkey no records were kept on the history of native dogs. Accounts written by travelers over the centuries tell of seeing large dogs used by shepherds. Archaeological finds indicate that dogs have been domesticated in that region of the world for many centuries. Sheep guard dogs of the Akbash type may well be among the oldest types of domestic dogs.

The argument—and there is plenty of argument—is this: Is the Akbash one of the many types of large sheep-guarding dogs, and a distinct breed, or merely a white version of a sheep guardian long known in Turkey? Some Akbash supporters believe their breed is a cross between a large Mastiff type and a speedy hunting dog known as the Turkish Greyhound. Like most arguments about the early history of dog breeds, this one will never be settled. And it doesn't really make any difference, for whatever its early history, the Akbash Dog is a magnificent animal and a very distinct one. Though it is quite new to America, it has proved to be remarkably adaptable to conditions very different from those found in its homeland.

Akbash Dogs come from a small area of western Turkey, which is still remote and primitive. They are used to guard flocks of sheep and goats from wolves, jackals, and other predators.

The powerful and graceful white dog came to the attention of David and Judith Nelson, Americans who were living in Turkey. They took a puppy into the country home they had rented, though local shepherds warned them it would never adapt to being a house pet. Much to everyone's surprise, the puppy adapted beautifully. Then the Nelsons were warned that when the puppy grew up it would turn vicious. It didn't. So they brought the Akbash Dog home with them when they returned to the United States. They went back to Turkey several times to obtain additional breeding stock.

The Akbash Dog was developed for guarding sheep and goats, not for herding them, moving them from place to place. They are natural guardians, and will become very attached to and protect whatever it is they are raised with—sheep, goats, horses, cats, or people.

David Sims and Orysia Dawydiak raise and train Akbash Dogs on their farm on Prince Edward Island in Canada. They say that the dogs tend to prefer goats to sheep, because the goats are livelier and will play with the dogs, while sheep are boring. Most of the dogs like people best. "After all, they know where the good times are!" say the couple. Akbash Dogs have even been known to make deep attachments to chickens or exotic birds.

"We've seen several instances where young guard dogs have 'stolen' newborn lambs from their mothers and tried to play mother themselves. . . . Even our indoor pet Akbash male has adopted lambs that we brought into the house to revive after a tough or cold delivery. He cuddles them, licks them, and cleans them, and he will growl at any dog or cat that approaches 'his' lamb."

The Akbash is a large dog, with males weighing up to 130 pounds and females as much as 100 pounds. That makes it a little larger than the Great Pyrenees, the recognized breed that the Akbash most resembles, and only a little smaller than the giant St. Bernard. They are all-white dogs with possibly a little very light brown or biscuit color on the ears. They have a heavy double-coat and any potential owner should be warned that this dog sheds a lot.

Despite its size, and the fact that not too many years ago it was guarding sheep in the mountains of Turkey, the Akbash has fitted in remarkably well to life in modern America. Obviously a dog of this size is not suitable for a small city apartment. But they can do well in a fair-sized house, so long as they are given adequate exercise.

While they are excellent guardians, and very wary of strangers, the Akbash is not an overly aggressive or vicious dog. They will not attack unless directly threatened. They also do not bark excessively. These dogs are calm, intelligent, and highly trainable. They are big dogs, and they are guard dogs; if they are to become the trusted family pet, they must be trained properly, and they must be socialized from puppyhood. That means they have to get used to people and other dogs.

The Akbash has been lucky. In its native Turkey the ancient and traditional methods of sheep and goat herding are in decline. Inevitably, the number of dogs used to guard the herds will also decline. But the dog has found a number of enthusiastic and responsible supporters in North America. They are intent not only on promoting the breed but making sure that the dogs are the best they can possibly be. The stately Akbash Dog seems destined for greater popularity in this part of the world. It's rare now, but it won't always be.

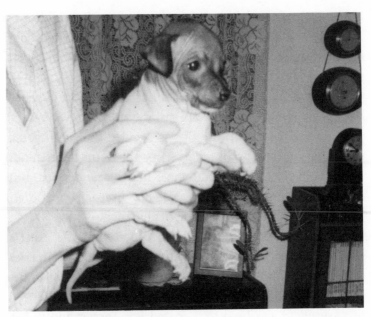

American Hairless Terrier puppy

2. The American Hairless Terrier

The United States can boast its very own breed of hairless dog. Very few countries can. The American version of a hairless dog is also the newest hairless dog to appear in the world. Named the American Hairless Terrier, it's an extremely important little animal. That's because hairlessness is a mutation (an instant genetic change) and it's almost impossible to pinpoint precisely when a mutation occurs. Yet we know the exact date this particular mutation appeared. The first American Hairless Terrier was born on August 12, 1972.

The little pink-and-black female was born into a litter of Rat Terriers. Rat Terriers are small, smooth-coated dogs originally bred to go after rats. When Edwin and Willie Scott of Trout, Louisiana, were given the hairless pup as a gift, they were delighted. They named her Josephine and called her Jo for short. She was an instant star everywhere she went and so much fun the Scotts decided the world could use some more dogs like her. They made up their minds they would try to develop a whole new hairless breed. But how? They were dog owners, not dog breeders, and their knowledge of genetics was practically zilch.

The Scotts tried speaking with experts but the experts weren't much help. Most said the Scotts' bald pet terrier was a one-of-a-kind creature, a fluke of nature, a not-to-be-repeated accident. The Scotts decided to go ahead and breed Jo anyway. Jo was bred to a coated Rat Terrier and in her very first litter there was a hairless female. The Scotts thought the new breed was on its way, but they soon learned that it was only a case of beginners' luck. Using good sense, care, and always keeping an eye on Jo's health, they continued to breed her. But each new litter produced only dogs with fur.

The Scotts were about ready to give up any hope of developing a new hairless breed when Jo surprised them. She was nine years old and down to her very last litter when she gave birth to both a hairless female and a hairless male. It was cause for celebration!

Now the Scotts were about to launch a solid carefully planned breeding program. The result was good healthy pups. Unlike many other hairless breeds, these hairless canines usually have a full set of teeth and unblemished skin. And except for brows and whiskers, the American Hairless

Terrier, as the Scotts dubbed their new breed, is as hairless as an egg. Whatever hair the pups are born with is quickly shed over a period of weeks.

Like all terriers, American Hairless Terriers are lively, active, wide-awake dogs. When full-grown, they weigh between seven and twelve pounds and stand nine to thirteen-and-a-half inches at the shoulder. Their ears are erect, their tail can be long or short. They are born with large black or brown spots on their skin and get more but smaller spots as they mature. Their skin tends to darken over the years.

Though the dog is still extremely rare, the Scotts have their very own kennel called Trout Creek Kennels. The American Hairless Terrier is their specialty. They've done it, created a new hairless breed. Now their dream come true has caught the fancy of scientists and veterinarians, experts who can see the importance of studying these small hairless dogs for what they can tell us about genetics. And the Scotts, true to their dream of creating a healthy new hairless breed, have kept excellent records.

Argentine Dogo puppy

3. The Argentine Dogo

Back in the 1940s and '50s there was a popular comic book character called Captain Marvel. The lame newsboy Billy Batson had only to utter the magic word "SHAZAM" to be transformed into the caped superhero Captain Marvel. The magic word stood for the qualities that Captain Marvel was supposed to possess: the wisdom of <u>S</u>olomon, the strength of <u>H</u>ercules, the stamina of <u>A</u>tlas, the power of <u>Z</u>eus, the courage of <u>A</u>chilles, the speed of <u>M</u>ercury: SHAZAM.

The Argentine Dogo's magic word might be "CBIGDS" or

something even longer and more unpronounceable. This unique animal is the result of one man's attempt to produce a superior hunting dog, by combining the qualities of many different breeds.

Back in the 1920s, Dr. Antonio Nores Martinez of Argentina wanted to develop a dog that would be good for hunting big game, like wild boar and jaguar. Big game hunting in Argentina in those days was not like hunting in America, or practically anywhere else. The hunter pursued his prey accompanied by his dogs and armed only with a large knife. This phase of the hunt was called the *"monteria."* Dr. Martinez wanted a dog that could track the game and hold it until the hunter arrived.

The first requirement for such a dog was that it be big, strong, tough, and fearless. Dr. Martinez was well acquainted with such a dog. It was called the Old Fighting Dog of Cordova. This was a type of dog bred specifically for dog fighting. It was usually a cross between a Bull Terrier and a Spanish Mastiff, or one of the old fighting bulldogs of England.

Such a dog, however, presented real problems in hunting. In order to be a good hunter a dog must be able to work in a group or pack. The Cordova dogs were so fierce and aggressive that they would immediately attack one another. Since they were strictly fighting dogs, they didn't need, or possess, the good sense of smell a hunter needs to track prey.

So Dr. Martinez set out to create his own hunting dog. He bred the basic Cordova dog stock to Boxers in order to tone down the fighting dog's aggressive nature and make it more stable and trainable. The huge Irish Wolfhound was used to improve the dog's speech, size, and sight hunting.

13

The Great Pyrenees was bred into the line to give the dog the ability to thrive in all sorts of climates, and to accentuate its white color, very helpful for a dog that was used for hunting in thick underbrush where it might be hard for the hunter to keep track of him. The Dogue de Bordeaux added strength, particularly jaw strength. The rugged Spanish Mastiff was bred back into the line for overall vigor and stamina. Put them all together and you get "CBIGDS." There were actually a couple of other dogs that contributed to the development of this breed—the Pointer, to improve its scenting ability, the Great Dane, to make the dog taller. The result was the Argentine Dogo—the only breed of dog ever developed in Argentina.

The Dogo is a large, sleek-looking dog standing twenty-four to twenty-seven inches high at the shoulder and weighing up to 100 pounds. The fur is white. Occasionally puppies

Java Del Borinquen, ten-month-old female Dogo

are born with a spot or two of color, but the all-white Dogo is considered the best by breeders. The fur is also short, and they are more tolerant of extreme heat than cold. That's what you would expect from a dog that comes from a hot climate.

It's unlikely that anyone in the United States is going to go big game hunting with a pack of Dogos and a knife. In this country the Dogo is used primarily as a guard dog, and a family companion. Considering that the Dogo's basic stock was a vicious fighting dog, and the breed itself is less than seventy-five years old, the Argentine Dogo is a remarkably stable, trustworthy, and trainable animal. In Argentina they are sometimes used as Seeing-Eye dogs, a good indication of just how intelligent and trainable this breed really is. Dogo owners are extremely anxious that their breed does not get a reputation for fighting or unwarranted aggressiveness.

Still, the Argentine Dogo is a large and very strong animal, with deep-seated protective instincts. They have a loud bark, and growl fiercely, often curling back their lips and displaying their teeth. That's generally enough to frighten off any intruder. They will attack strangers, and they must get basic obedience training, and have a lot of contact with people and other dogs from the time they are puppies.

Dogo owners are particularly proud of their breed as a family dog. They say it is exceptionally good with children, and will put up with a great deal of tail pulling and ear tugging from children in the family. In Argentina it has a reputation as being a good babysitter.

The Argentine Dogo is a real newcomer to the United States. It's hard to get, and prices for a good specimen remain high, but the Dogo has a core of devoted supporters who are dedicated to the task of getting this handsome and sturdy breed better known. The Dogo's most enthusiastic and energetic booster is Graciela Hoff, a native of Buenos Aires, Argentina, who now lives in Puerto Rico. Dogs from her Borinquen Kennels can now be found throughout the Caribbean, and in many parts of the United States.

"My dream," she says, "is to have this breed recognized by the American Kennel Club. One day I want to sit in the stands at the Westminster [dog show] and watch a beautiful and elegant Argentine Dogo gait around the ring."

Berdot's Tony, a five-month-old Bolognese

4. The Bolognese

The Bolognese is a lap dog, but a lap dog that has sat on some of the most glamorous and powerful laps in history. The list of dukes and duchesses, counts and countesses, who owned Bolognese in the Age of Kings reads like an historical "Who's Who." In the eighteenth century France's elegant Marquise de Pompadour was devoted to her pet Bolognese. Catherine the Great, monarch of Russia, was enchanted with the breed. The little toy dog was the prized possession of European nobility as far back as the Renaissance. Bred first in Bologna, Italy, the dog may have begun its climb to fame and fortune as early as the eleventh and twelfth centuries.

The Bolognese is a member of an ancient group of small dogs known as the Bichon group, which evolved in the Mediterranean region of Europe. It was the last of the Bichons to arrive in America. Not until 1987 was a Bolognese imported to the United States and so far very few of these delightful little dogs live on this side of the Atlantic Ocean. But just as the AKC-registered Bichon Frise is conquering America and the rare breed Bichon named the Havanese is about to make a run for it, so the merry little Bolognese has a good chance of becoming a canine superstar someday. Just wait till people see it and get to know it. As puppies, Bolognese are cuter than a whole toy store full of stuffed animals, and when they grow up they are charming as well as beautiful.

Good with children, devoted to their owners, they are friendly but quick to bark at intruders. Bolognese are sturdy playful dogs that stand ten to twelve inches at the shoulder and weigh from ten to twelve pounds. The dog has furry dropped ears and large expressive dark eyes with fluffy tufts of ringlets covering the dog's entire body. The dogs need a lot of brushing to keep their coats from matting. Because the Bolognese coat is so lovely, owners don't mind the work.

Such a luxurious-looking little dog would have seemed absolutely right in a palace, a fit companion to an aristocrat. Queen Maria Theresa of Austria considered her pretty Bolognese such a jewel of a dog that she couldn't bear to part with it after it died and had a taxidermist preserve it. The dog is still around. You can see it, stuffed and mounted, in the Museum of Natural History in Vienna.

Sadly, though the Bolognese prospered in the Age of

World Champion Bolognese, Igor of Belgium

Kings, when royalty vanished the dogs almost vanished with them. But there were enough admirers of the Bolognese in Italy and Belgium to save the breed. Why Belgium? In 1688 Cosimo de Medici sent eight Bolognese to Belgium from Italy and the dogs became the pets of wealthy families living in the city of Brussels. The Belgians never stopped loving the Bolognese and today Belgian bloodlines are the best in the world. Bolognese from Belgium are highly sought after by breeders everywhere. Thanks to the efforts of their loyal fans, Bolognese like Igor and Elaine in Belgium, Lilly in Italy, and Tony and Lucy in Colorado are thriving today.

Canaan Dogs named Spatterdash Dreidle and Spatterdash Limor

5. The Canaan Dog

There are a lot of good things to say about the Canaan Dog. For starters, it's hardy, intelligent, exceptionally long-lived, a good companion, and a good protector. You can hardly ask more of a dog than that. The only breed native to Israel, Canaans were originally used by the ancient Hebrews as herding dogs and they still have strong herding instincts. The dogs can even boast a particularly glamorous legend. The Biblical Queen Jezebel is said to have kept a Canaan Dog tied to her throne with a leash of gold.

After the Romans defeated and dispersed the Hebrews, Canaan Dogs escaped to the Negev Desert where they became feral (wild) animals. They had to be healthy and tough to survive desert life. As centuries passed, some of the dogs found their way to the camps of nomadic Arabs who used them to guard livestock.

The story of the modern Canaan Dog really begins in the 1930s and involves a woman named Dr. Rudophina Menzel. She was a world-famous expert on canine behavior who had trained dogs to work with the Austrian police. Dr. Menzel was Jewish and when the Nazi era dawned in the 1930s, she fled Europe and went to the land now called Israel. War was brewing there too and the newly organized Israeli Defense Force needed dogs to help guard isolated Jewish settlements. To help the Israeli Defense Force, Dr. Menzel decided to domesticate and train the wild Canaan Dog because it was strong, hardy, and used to the harsh local climate. It was also right there on the scene, living in packs.

It was no easy task, luring wild dogs and training them. It took Dr. Menzel years, but she succeeded and Canaans played a vital role in the Israeli War for Independence. Canaans are not only used by the military in Israel today, they are also used as Seeing-Eye guide dogs for the blind. Most commonly, they are family watchdogs and pets.

Packs of feral Canaans still roam wild in parts of Israel, but each year there are fewer and fewer of them. A concerned Israeli government is doing everything it can to save these wild dogs. Israeli Canaan breeders even use the wild dogs in their breeding programs. They believe the wild dogs add strength to the breed as a whole. Canaan breeders in the United States have a very different attitude. They want AKC approval and that means the American version of the Israeli

Spatterdash Dreidle

dog has to be a stable breed, well-established, with a well-documented background.

The first Canaan reached America in 1965 and there are several hundred Canaans in the United States today. Not only do they compete in rare breed shows, but you'll find them in obedience and tracking events, where they shine. The Canaan Dog is a good learner, easy to train.

Canaans are also very loyal dogs who adore their owners.

Alert and extremely protective of their territory, they are quick to spot an approaching stranger and quick to bark when that stranger enters property Canaans consider theirs. They are not vicious or aggressive attack dogs, but the sight of a Canaan or two circling around you suspiciously, ready to bite if necessary, ought to be enough to drive away any unwanted intruder. When a Canaan leaves home, owner in tow, however, the dog is merely aloof. Away from its territory, it won't warm up to strangers but it won't bother them either. Living in packs comes naturally to Canaans and many Canaan owners have more than one dog. The Canaans get on just fine with one another, but woe to any strange canine who invades their territory.

Although Canaans bark only when there's a reason, they do more than bark. They have such a wide range of sounds they practically sing. They also love to dig holes. If you ever own a Canaan Dog you'll discover that they dig a hole every chance they get.

When it comes to looks, the Canaan Dog has a neat, sensibly smart appearance. It's built to be practical. Medium-sized, it stands nineteen to twenty-four inches at the shoulder, has a wedge-shaped head, upright ears, a harsh outer coat, and a short undercoat. The dog should be trim, muscular, athletically agile, and move at a quick trot. A Canaan has slightly slanted eyes, eyes interested in everything it sees. Canaans can be sandy colored, red-brown, white, or black. Dogs with large areas of white on their bodies are preferred.

Canaan Dog owners often give their prized animals charming names like Dreidel (a children's toy top with Hebrew letters), Ariel, and Bagel. Bagel's our favorite name. How could you help but fall in love with a dog named Bagel?

Char-Lea, a Catahoula Leopard Dog

6. The Catahoula Leopard Dog

When is a dog not a dog? Why, when it's a Cat—a Catahoula Leopard Dog, that is. The Cat, as its proud owners have nicknamed it, is one very special animal. If what you're after is some cute little ball of fluff or a fancy show dog that's got to be groomed twenty times a day and eats only T-bone steaks or tofu, then forget the Cat. He's a hardy "workin' dawg," at home in the swampy heat of Louisiana. The Cat's fans, and there are a lot of them, wouldn't want it any other way.

Catahoula Leopard Dog breeders like to ride around in pickup trucks filled with a litter or two of Cat pups. They like hot spicy Cajun food. They like to brag about the Cat getting dubbed the official state dog of Louisiana. The Cat was voted that title by the Louisiana State Legislature.

Cat owners will tell you about the big anniversary party held five years later to celebrate that day in 1979 when the Cat was named top dog. At the party Louisiana Governor Edwin Edwards was given a Cat puppy. Governor Edwards also received a copy of an album recorded by country western singer Gene Simmons called "Louisiana Catahoula Cur State Dog." Seems right. If the Cat listened to music, it would be country western.

Our dictionary defines cur as a "mongrel dog, especially a worthless or unfriendly one." Many dog breeders would shudder at the idea of their dog being called a cur, as in Louisiana Catahoula Cur State Dog. Not Catahoula breeders. They don't even mind another name given their dogs, Coward Dogs. Catahoulas won the label "Coward Dogs" because of their style of hunting wild hogs and working domesticated hogs.

Hog dogs (as Cats trained for hog work are called) bark and snap at the hogs, then turn and run. This may look cowardly, but it's really just plain smart. Turning tail and running is the Cat's way of getting the hogs to chase them. The hogs chase the dogs right out of the swamp into the open, sometimes all the way to their pens. The Cat can also be trained to hunt other animals besides hogs, such as deer, and to herd cattle. Cats who help cowboys round up cattle are called cow dogs.

But back to that dictionary definition of cur. True, the Cat is very, very unfriendly to strangers. It's a trait that makes the Cat a tough guard dog. But Cats are anything but unfriendly to their owners. In the heart of their own family, Cats are loyal, playful, and affectionate to both adults and children.

As for being mongrels, yes, there was a time when serious dog breeders ignored the Cat. But that's no longer the case. In 1977 the National Association of Louisiana Catahoulas (NALC) was founded. By 1984 NALC's certified breeders had established the first official breed standard. Thanks to NALC, the Catahoula has come a very long way in the past decade. NALC registers pure-breed Cats, keeps records, sponsors conformation dog shows, field trials, and junior showmanship classes. Cats may indeed be "workin' dawgs," but thanks to NALC, there are plenty of handsome Cats standing tall in the show ring, tail held high.

Certainly no one who knows the breed would consider a Cat worthless, no matter what the dictionary has to say about curs. As long as he's well cared for, has room to run, and is kept under solid control, a Cat will do just about anything you'd expect a dog to do. A Cat's hearing, sense of smell, and eyesight are first-rate. Catahoulas have webbed feet and so are good swimmers. What's more, they take to obedience training as easily as they take to water. Cats are famous for learning tricks quickly.

When it comes to looks, the Catahoula is a rangy dog with slick, short hair. Size-wise, you'd place the Cat in the medium to medium-large range. Females measure twenty to twenty-four inches at the shoulder, while males measure twenty-two to twenty-six inches. A Catahoula can weigh anywhere from fifty to ninety-five pounds, but should always be trim, muscular, strong, and agile. Working dogs need stamina and endurance. The Cat has plenty of both. Though a Cat isn't full-grown until the age of two, he's ready for work when he's only nine months old.

One of the first things you'll notice about a Cat is the way he likes to flop down like a junkyard dog, then go slinking around with his tail between his legs. The very first thing you'll notice about him are his eyes. Cats have weird eyes. A Catahoula Leopard Dog's eyes can be brown or green, but many have white (called glass) eyes. Cats often have one colored eye and one glass eye. Cats may even have spots of white in one or both eyes. These spots are called glass cracks. Having both eyes white—called double glass eyes—is a big plus for a show dog. That's because glass eyes have an eerie kind of beauty.

The Leopard in a Catahoula Leopard Dog's name comes from the spots in the dog's coat. Not all Cats are spotted. Some have solid-colored coats, though most have at least

Trooper, a three-year-old male Catahoula Leopard Dog

some white trim. But it's the spotted dogs—the Leopards—that are really something to see. A single Leopard's spots may come in as many as two to five different colors. Cats come in a wide range of base coat colors, too. The king of Cats in the show ring is a big-boned, white-trimmed, blue Leopard with double glass eyes. He's a breeder's dream.

Where did this strange-looking dog come from? Catahoula is an Indian word meaning "beautiful clear water," and the Catahoula Leopard Dog originated in the Catahoula Lakes region of central Louisiana. In the sixteenth century Spanish conquerors reached the region. They brought strong Mastiffs with them which were used as war dogs. Legend has it that the Indians helped care for Mastiffs wounded in battle who were left behind by the Spanish.

The Indians had their own dogs which they bred to the Mastiffs. From this mix came a white-eyed, spotted dog which later settlers named the Catahoula. In the years that followed, the breed spread to Texas and other parts of the South and Southwest. Today the Cat is found in other sections of the country as well. Cat owners consider their dog to be an important native American breed. They feel downright down-home patriotic about him.

If you want to know more about the Catahoula Leopard Dog, get in touch with NALC, a dog club with a sense of humor. You may be interested in the many souvenirs the organization has for sale, such as Cat bumper stickers, posters, T-shirts, and baseball hats. NALC also puts out a delightfully funny newsletter totally devoted to Louisiana's own number-one prize dog.

Cavalier King Charles Spaniels

7. The Cavalier King Charles Spaniel

Friends and admirers of the seventeenth-century English kings, Charles I and Charles II, were called cavaliers. Originally the word cavalier meant a knight on horseback, and certainly the seventeenth-century cavaliers were aristocrats. Both kings and cavaliers were fond of a charming breed of small Spaniel and often posed with their dogs when they had their portraits painted. These little dogs, which can be seen romping through many a painting of that era, have been dubbed the Cavalier King Charles Spaniel. They richly deserve their royal name.

Royal they may be, but snobbish they are not. Oh, they may be a bit dignified around strangers but they love their owners. Cavaliers (as they are called for short) just have to be part of the family or they become very unhappy. There's no reason why they shouldn't be part of the family. They have a nice steady temperament. They're affectionate and playful. Anyone who's ever owned a Cavalier will tell you they're a joy to be around.

Though they are toy dogs, they are also Spaniels, descendants of sporting dogs. Your average Cavalier may not do much hunting nowadays but he's certainly not lazy or clinging. Cavaliers enjoy a long walk, a swim, a day's jaunt in the woods, and they need regular daily exercise. Because they're only twelve to thirteen inches at the shoulder and weigh between thirteen and eighteen pounds, they can be as active and lively as they want. Owning an energetic Cavalier is not like owning an energetic eighty-pound dog. Cavaliers can live comfortably in an apartment as well as a house. They manage nicely if they have a fenced-in yard.

Don't think Cavaliers are always on the move. They like to ride in the car, curl up in your lap, and since they're highly intelligent and want to please, they do well in obedience training. They get along extremely well with one another and owners often have at least a pair and sometimes a whole crowd of Cavaliers. These gentle dogs get along well with children, too, but kids must understand that the dogs are toy-sized. You can play with them, but you should never be too rough with them.

Though the Cavalier was once the pet of kings, as aristocratic tastes changed it fell out of favor. Pugs, toy dogs with pushed-in faces and bulging eyes, came into fashion. The English Toy Spaniel, which may have Pug in its back-

Tessa, a Cavalier King Charles Spaniel

ground, eclipsed the Cavalier. The English Toy Spaniel is a delicate dog standing nine to ten inches at the shoulder and weighing nine to twelve pounds. It has a domelike head and protruding eyes. In contrast, the Cavalier's head is slightly rounded but not domed, and because its ears are set high on the sides of its head, the head looks flat. Its muzzle is

31

much longer than the English Toy Spaniel's, making it a nosey little animal. Its face is longer. Its large lustrous dark eyes are set well apart but aren't bulgy.

By the late nineteenth century the English Toy Spaniel type was in, and the Cavalier was out. Cavaliers weren't exhibited at dog shows. Breeding records weren't kept. And there was no breed standard. If the breed wasn't extinct it was on the edge of extinction.

Then in 1926 an American named Roswell Eldridge decided he just had to own one of the beautiful Spaniels of the old type he had seen in the paintings of such famous artists as Van Dyke, Gainsborough, and Watteau. Mr. Eldridge went to England in search of the dog of his dreams. When he got there and couldn't find any he offered a large sum of money to any breeder who could find him one. He made the offer through an ad placed in a dog show catalog. The show was Crufts, England's best dog show. The ad created a big stir.

Most breeders ignored Mr. Eldridge, but the ad set others thinking. Maybe it was sad that the old-style little Spaniel was gone. Perhaps the breed should be revived. Enough people were convinced to set to work and in 1928 the Cavalier King Charles Spaniel Club was started in England. Now, many years later, the little Spaniel seen in the old paintings is back, as irresistible as ever. In England it is registered with the English Kennel Club and has become one of the most popular of all toy breeds.

It wasn't until 1956 that the Cavalier King Charles Spaniel Club was formed in America, and in 1962 the dog was accepted into the Miscellaneous Class of the AKC. Today there are several thousand Cavaliers in our country and some breeders worry that the dog may be en route to becoming too popular. Since full AKC recognition would bring even more attention, some breeders want the Cavaliers to remain in the Miscellaneous Class.

It's not that the breeders mind more people seeing or even owning the dogs. It's that they fear people who don't understand sound breeding practices will begin breeding Cavaliers once the dogs become popular. Poor breeding practices can harm the health of a breed and lower its overall quality.

If you ever meet a Cavalier you'll see why breeders care so much about the dog. It's a graceful well-balanced animal with long ears covered with feathery silky hair. It has a long silky, sometimes wavy, soft coat. It has noticeably furry feet. The dog looks like it's walking around in bedroom slippers.

The dog has beautiful markings and beautiful color. Cavaliers can be jet black with tan markings or they may be a solid rich ruby red. There are black-and-white Cavaliers with tan markings. There are Cavaliers with bright chestnut-colored markings on a pearly white base. These chestnut-and-white dogs sometimes have a spot on their head located right between their ears which is considered a plus in the show ring.

The Cavalier King Charles Spaniel looks like it's fit for a king. It's fit for a lot of just plain ordinary people, too.

Dark Star, a Chinese Crested Hairless puppy

8. The Chinese Crested

Picture a dog with a flowing crest or knot of hair—either between its ears or all over its head—sox of fur on its feet, a long plume of fur on its tail, and no hair at all on the rest of its body. Unusual? You bet. The Hairless version of the Chinese Crested, and that's what you've just pictured, is definitely an out-of-the-ordinary kind of dog.

What does the dog's skin feel like? Soft, smooth, velvety, and lovely to stroke or touch. The dog can be any one of a number of colors: blue, pink, lavender, honey, red, white, or black. The dog's skin may be spotted or even speckled. This slender little canine with a graceful deerlike body rarely weighs more than ten pounds, often weighs as little as five or seven, and stands no more than twelve or thirteen inches at the shoulders.

But wait! Now picture a dog similar in shape and size but with a soft silky coat of hair covering its entire body. This, too, is a Chinese Crested. The furred variety of the breed goes by the charming name of Powderpuff. With one exception, Hairless and Powderpuff puppies can be born in the same litter. The exception is when Powderpuffs are bred to Powderpuffs. Then no Hairless pups will be born. At dog shows Hairless and Powderpuffs are shown separately.

Where in the world did such a special breed of dogs come from? Despite the "Chinese" in their name, many experts believe most hairless breeds originated in Africa and/or Mexico and South America. The label "Chinese" stuck to this particular breed because for centuries they were prized in China. Some of the dogs bred there were delicate, like the modern Crested, but there was another stocky, heavier kind of Crested bred there, too, with a "cobby" body type. There are probably no Cresteds at all in China anymore, cobby or otherwise.

We don't know just when Chinese Cresteds first reached America but over a century ago, in 1885, two Cresteds turned up at the Westminster Dog Show in New York, then and now the premier dog show in America. In the years that followed, Cresteds were rarely shown and there was no written standard to point the way, so the AKC dropped the dogs in 1965.

There was no national Chinese Crested Club in our country back then either. Thanks to a few dedicated breeders,

Champion Gipez's Shu-Chi of Sun-A-Ra, first Best in Show Powderpuff in the United States

everything changed within a few years and things began to look brighter for the Crested. A club was formed. The dogs were registered with the club. Today there's a strict formal written standard for the Crested and a number of excellent breeders are devoted to these very special little dogs.

Actually, Cresteds are by far and away the most popular of all the hairless breeds in America and they have returned to the AKC, at least in the Miscellaneous Class. Owners and breeders are eager for full recognition and since interest in the breed keeps right on growing they have every reason to be hopeful.

To be a Chinese Crested breeder you have to know your way around genetics. That's because hairlessness carries with it certain problems. Take teeth. Hairless Cresteds don't have a full set of teeth. Powderpuffs do. Because the Powderpuff enriches the overall health of the breed in many ways, they are a vital part of any sound breeding program. And that goes even for breeders most interested in producing and showing the hairless variety of the dog.

Because they're so unusual, Cresteds are very interesting. Hairless Cresteds can get sunburned. They also tan. It's not at all unusual for a Crested's skin to change color and for the dog to grow darker as it goes through life. Because sunlight affects them so much, owners have to make sure the dogs don't get too much sun. This is one dog that needs to get into the shade when it's outside.

Although the body temperature of a Hairless Crested is a few degrees higher than the body temperature of most dogs, cool breezes are definitely not for them. This is an animal that needs warmth. Not that they can't live in cold climates. They can and do. It's just that they need special protection. Because the dogs tend to get blackheads, pimples, and other skin irritations, they need a lot of baths. Many owners rub oil into their dog's skin because oil helps keep the Hairless Crested's skin soft and smooth. Owners sometimes put sweaters on their dogs, but they have to be careful. Itchy fabrics like wool can really bother the sensitive skin of a Hairless Chinese Crested.

Have these dogs ever been put to work? In a sense, yes. People once used these little dogs to keep warm. Live heating pads, they were plopped down on an aching human shoulder, sore joint, or sore back that needed healthy warmth. In turn, these little dogs seem to enjoy cuddling up to people, maybe partly because people are warm, too. But the main reason they're so affectionate is sheer friendliness. Both the Hairless and the Powderpuff have very nice temperaments. They also have beautiful dark almond-shaped eyes and enjoy gazing soulfully up at their owners. Some people claim the dogs seem to smile and can even shed real tears. The dogs also have very agile paws. There are owners who say their dogs can actually hold a pencil in their paws or embrace people in a rather humanlike hug.

And how does the Crested get along with children? Well, they're great with kids, the right kids, that is. This is one dog that can't be handled roughly. If it's love you want from a pet, though, the Crested is little, its heart is big. When it comes to love, the Chinese Crested has plenty of love to give.

Dual Champion Redbone Coonhound, Little Man

9. The Coonhounds

In 1770 George Washington imported Foxhounds from England. Later he was given French hounds by the Marquis de Lafayette. It is believed that some of these dogs were the foundation stock for today's Coonhounds. One of Washington's descendants, George Washington Maupin, and another man, John W. Walker, are credited with developing the popular breed now known as the Treeing Walker Coonhound.

Coonhounds are generally identified with the South, but

they can be found in rural areas of practically every state. These are the dogs that Elvis sang about.

How can so famous, fabled, common, and intensely an American dog be classed as a rare breed? Simple. The Coonhounds—with the exception of one breed, the Black and Tan Coonhound—are not recognized by the American Kennel Club. And that's the way Coonhound owners want it. They can't see their hounds parading around the show ring at Madison Square Garden with the Poodles and Pomeranians. These dogs have names like Tarheel Jake, Timber Chopper Rocky, and Blue Bullet.

Coonhounds, however, are not just any old barnyard mongrel. Six distinct breeds of Coonhounds are registered with the United Kennel Club (UKC).

There are definite appearance standards for the Coonhounds, just as there are for AKC-registered dogs, and today careful pedigree records are kept. Coonhound owners are more interested in performance than appearance and pedigree, however. So it's the hunting trials sponsored by the UKC and other organizations, rather than the shows, that are really important to the people who raise and train these dogs.

Coonhounds are, as the name implies, primarily used for hunting raccoons. The hound picks up the coon's scent, and follows it until it catches the coon on the ground or more commonly chases it up a tree. It then stands at the bottom of the tree making a lot of noise until the hunter shows up. Coonhounds have been used to hunt other game as well—opossums, bobcats, and occasionally bears and even mountain lions.

Most Coonhounds are descended from English Foxhounds. You've probably seen pictures of a fox hunt. The pack of hounds chases the fox across an open field. Behind the hounds come the elegantly dressed hunters on horseback. The horses gallop along gracefully, jumping stone walls and wooden fences.

Coon hunting is a bit different. For one thing it's usually done at night. The hunters are likely to be wearing bib overalls, checkered shirts, and caps with a Jim Beam logo. The scene of the hunt is a forest or even a swampy area. The hunters follow their dogs on foot, though occasionally they will ride a mule. A full-tilt gallop on horseback through a forest at night is not a recommended activity.

The hunter keeps track of his dogs by the sounds they make. Coonhounds bark or bay almost constantly when on a trail, and when they tree their quarry they have a different sort of bark.

In times gone by, hunting enthusiasts would become quite poetic about the sounds that their dogs would make. "The hounds all join in glorious cry," wrote Henry Fielding back in the eighteenth century. Others spoke of the "music of the hounds."

Coonhunters, too, can be quite enthusiastic about their dogs' voices, though they are a little less poetic than the old-time English foxhunter. Coonhunters call a dog's voice its "mouth" and they talk about some dogs having a "good deep bawl" or a "bugle mouth." A dog that makes a lot of noise is said to be a "free tonguer" and when the quarry is treed, the sound can change to a "steady chop."

Of the Coonhounds popular in America the largest is the Black and Tan. This is the one Coonhound breed that is recognized by the AKC, and it can be seen at many large dog shows, though these are still primarily working dogs rather than show dogs.

Blue Muffin, four-year-old Bluetick Coonhound female

The Bluetick Coonhound is a predominately dark gray dog with black spots, and some tan on the face and feet. It's a good-sized dog, with a large male weighing up to eighty-five pounds, and probably has the best mouth of all the Coonhounds. Its voice can be heard for miles. It's a rugged muscular breed that is adapted to hunting under a wide variety of conditions.

When the English Coonhound was first registered with the UKC in 1905, it was under the name of the English Fox and Coonhound. In England this dog's ancestors were used mainly for fox hunting. But the dog was gradually adapted to the much rougher American terrain and climate, and is now used primarily for coon hunting. This hound can come in any one of a variety of colors, usually white with a reddish saddle and red ticking or small spots. In some areas it is called a Redtick Coonhound. As with the other Coonhounds, performance in the field, not appearance, is what counts.

In the early days of coonhunting practically any reddish dog who could hunt was called "Redbone." Then a few serious breeders decided to produce a dog that would always be true to the type in color, build, and temperament. It was registered with the UKC in 1902, the second Coonhound to be recognized. Today Redbone is generally a solid red or reddish-brown dog, with perhaps a bit of white on the chest and feet. The Redbone is probably the most common of the Coonhounds in the Deep South, because it does not tolerate extreme cold very well.

The Treeing Walker Coonhound has one of the longest and oddest names in dogdom. The foundation stock for the breed is said to be a pack of English Foxhounds imported by Thomas Walker of Virginia in 1742. John W. Walker, a descendant of the original Walker, and George Washington's descendant helped to develop the breed. At least one major cross made in the nineteenth century strongly influenced the modern breed; strangely, it was a stolen dog from Tennessee called Tennessee Lead. Lead didn't look like the Virginia strain of English Foxhound, but he had an excellent tracking sense, unusual speed, and what is called a clean, short mouth. These were all qualities that Walker Hound breeders were looking for. Walker Hounds are so energetic that they have been known to actually climb trees in pursuit of their prey.

The Plott Hound is the only one of the Coonhounds that is not directly descended from the English Foxhound. It was developed from German dogs that had been used for hunting wild boar. The American dog is credited mainly to Jonathan Plott, who emigrated from Germany to the mountains of North Carolina in 1750, bringing some dogs from his native land with him. During the eighteenth century the original Plott Hounds were bred with what was called "leopard spotted bear dogs" in Georgia, and there may have been other crosses. The Plott Hound is known for its stamina and courage, and is said to have often served as a nursemaid and guardian for pioneer infants, while their mothers were off doing chores. The dogs are dark brown, streaked or striped with black. The Plott Hound is the least common of the Coonhound breeds because the Plott family rarely sold any of their dogs.

In addition to the six registered breeds of Coonhound, there are other Coonhound-type dogs, with names like Mountain Cur Dog, that have some local fame and loyal supporters.

Breeders and owners of these various dogs will argue endlessly as to which breed is best, and we wouldn't think of getting into the middle of that argument. Owners of different breeds will start by telling you that there's good and bad in all breeds, and then they will go on to explain to you how superior their particular breed is. Everybody has his own favorite training techniques as well.

Coonhunters like to sit around and tell stories about great hunts or great dogs of the past. Like fishermen, they may exaggerate a bit but there is a good deal of authentic dog history in the tales as well. In his history and memories of the Treeing Walker, Lester Nance writes about a traveling tobacco salesman named Duke Snell. Back in the 1920s Duke was staying in a hotel. Owners took the salesman out for a hunt with a large Walker-type dog they called Old Ring. Duke was so impressed by the dog's hunting skills that he decided to try and buy the animal next time he passed through the town. The trouble was, Ring didn't seem to have an owner. He had just wandered into town one day and stayed around for years. So Duke slipped the bellboy at the hotel two dollars to build a shipping crate. He put Old Ring into the crate and took him down to the railroad express office to ship him home. But the express man refused to take the crate, because he knew Old Ring, and had hunted with him several times, and just didn't want to see such a good dog leave town. So Duke had to go to the next town in order to ship Old Ring home.

In the years that followed it was said that Ring never once ran off track. Ring ultimately became the ancestor of the celebrated White River King—the first registered Treeing Walker. Now this dog could . . . but no, that's another story.

Treeing Walker Coonhound, Genessee Big Bucks

A well-trained Coonhound today can cost thousands of dollars. That's a lot more than Duke Snell slipped to the bellboy for Old Ring, even taking inflation into account.

Some of the larger Coonhounds are tough enough to take on a black bear, but in general the dogs are not aggressive to people or other dogs. Many are used to hunting cooperatively in packs, and unlike some other hunting breeds, the Coonhounds are strictly working dogs, and do not make good house pets. Hounds have a reputation for being lazy. Don't you believe it. All these dogs are extremely active, and if cooped up in a house for long they can be very destructive. They don't have a well-developed territorial sense, and are likely to run off at any time. If a hound picks up an interesting scent it's gone, paying no attention to roads or cars. In a highly populated area, that sort of dog won't survive for long. And even if it did manage to avoid being hit by a car, by the time the dog reached the end of its trail it would be thoroughly lost, and have no idea how to get home. Even well-trained hunting dogs may pick up the scent of a deer, or some other fast-moving prey, and have to be recovered miles from home and days later. When not actually hunting, most Coonhounds are kept kenneled or tied. Trying to keep a hound from chasing after any old game—trash, coonhunters call it—is one of the greatest training problems they have. "Is the dog trashy?" is the first question a prospective buyer might ask a Coonhound breeder.

Today most dogs in America are guardians, companions, family pets. The Coonhounds, however, remain pretty much what they were in George Washington's day—strictly working dogs. There are many things about modern America that Washington would not recognize. Coonhounds, though, would be familiar to him.

This Dogue de Bordeaux is named TNT's Chopper.

10. The Dogue de Bordeaux

Impressive—that's the best word to describe this powerfully built French Mastiff. Today's Dogue de Bordeaux is an even-tempered and highly prized companion, but it can look frightening. American Bordeaux breeder Peter Curley describes his champion Titan as having a face "only a mother could love." The Bordeaux's head is massive, and its jaws are tremendous. Yet Curley and other owners stress that

47

the Dogue is extremely trustworthy, and is particularly good with small children.

It wasn't always that way. The Dogue de Bordeaux, like most large dogs, has a violent history. There are many theories as to where this animal came from. Some say the breed's ancestors were brought to France from Asia by barbarian invaders over a thousand years ago. Others think the Dogues are descended from Roman war dogs. Still others suggest that they were originally the war dogs of the ancient Britons. No one really knows.

Whatever their origin, by the Middle Ages ancestors of these dogs were being used in France to hunt bears and wild boar. The Dogue's large size, power, and stubbornness made it useful for hunting such dangerous prey.

Dogues were also used in the arena as fighting dogs, pitted against bulls, bears, and other dogs. The Dogue de Bordeaux's fighting days were over long ago, but some of the old reputation clings to it. It's still called "The French Fighting Dog." In France an irritable person is said to have "a Dogue's temper." A person with an unpleasant or sour expression is described as having the "air of a Dogue."

By the end of the Middle Ages the Dogue de Bordeaux was also being used as a working dog. It guarded cattle and helped drive them to market. This job earned it the not-too-flattering nickname "the butcher's dog." The Dogue had another job, guarding the mansions and estates of the aristocrats. During the French Revolution, which started in 1789, many of the aristocrats were either killed or fled the country. Their guard dogs perished with them, and for a while it looked as if the Dogue de Bordeaux was on its way to becoming extinct.

A small number of the breed survived, particularly in the

Bordeaux region, and since that time French breeders have concentrated on breeding out the Dogue's aggressiveness, while keeping its qualities of loyalty, courage and, of course, its impressive size. In this they succeeded remarkably well.

Until recently the Dogue's popularity always suffered from competition with more well-known breeds such as the Boxer and Great Dane. Today it is still not a common breed even in France. But its popularity is growing, in France, throughout the rest of Europe, and in the United States.

Like its ancestors, the Bordeaux is a large dog. The males may stand at least twenty-six inches at the shoulder, and weigh 120 pounds and more. But they are not nervous or hyperactive animals, and they can adapt well to modern lifestyles. In France and Germany they are sometimes kept as pets in apartments, though a house with a well-fenced yard is preferable.

It's been a long, and often difficult, journey through history for the Dogue de Bordeaux. Finally, the future of this excellent dog seems secure.

Fila Champion, Ojeriza's Battle Cry

11. The Fila Brasileiro

The Fila Brasileiro is not a dog for everyone. In fact, it is a dog only for the experienced, devoted, and strong-willed dog owner. The Fila is a large, powerful, agile, and extremely aggressive animal. Other large breeds that are used as guard dogs, like the Doberman and the Rottweiler, have to be trained to attack. The Fila is a natural attack dog; it has to be trained *not* to attack. It displays this aggressive nature from the time it is a puppy.

June Zuber, a long-time dog breeder and trainer, wrote of her first Fila, a dog she nicknamed Baby:

"At six months I witnessed her protective nature and aggression. An acquaintance of mine dropped by one day while I had Baby outside for a leash training session. He came striding into the yard, and Baby watched him until he was approximately twenty feet away and then quietly stepped in front of me, putting her body at an angle to mine and dropped her head slightly, growling softly. I immediately tightened my grip on her leash and told my caller to stop where he was. I put my hand on her head and spoke gently to her, in a low but firm voice, to heel. She looked at me and then at my caller and then walked quietly with me to her kennel."

This, we will remind you, was a *six-month-old puppy*. That is an age when dogs that may become aggressive as adults are still playful. Not the Fila. Some puppies as young as two months will not allow themselves to be touched by strangers. When given a test for aggressiveness, the Fila always ranks right at the top.

In Brazil, where the Fila comes from, the official standard of the breed contains this startling sentence: "In the show ring, in general, he [the Fila] does not permit himself to be touched by the judge and if he attacks, his reaction should not be considered a fault but a corroboration of his temperament." The Brazilian standard says the Fila should display *ojeriza*, a Portuguese word which means adversion or hatred of strangers. And the Fila is a dog that weighs over 100 pounds, has huge jaws, and can clear a six-foot fence in a jump.

While working as a cattle-herding dog in Brazil, the Fila will instinctively go for a bull's cheeks or mouth. As a guard dog he may instinctively jump upward toward the intruder's throat. The name Fila may come from a Portuguese word meaning "to hold."

Why would anyone want such a dog?

Unfortunately some people want them for all the wrong reasons. There are those who get a sense of power from owning the biggest, fiercest dog around. These are the sort of people who shouldn't own any dog. There are others who believe that the fiercer the dog, the better protection it will be. The trouble is that unless a fierce dog is under complete control, it is far more likely to attack the postman, a neighbor's child, or even his owner than a potential burglar.

The true Filaphile—that is, the person who really loves and appreciates this breed—is not looking for a dangerous weapon with which to frighten others. He or she appreciates the dog's unique appearance, and legendary loyalty. "As loyal as a Fila" is an old Brazilian proverb. A well-trained Fila will follow his master anywhere, and is never happier than when lying with his head on his master's feet.

American Fila breeders stress that owning such a dog is a great responsibility and not one that should be undertaken lightly.

The Fila is a fairly recent import to the United States. Filas have only become known outside their native Brazil over the last ten or fifteen years. In Brazil most of the Filas are extremely fierce. Some still work on ranches where they are used to drive cattle and protect property. They are used as guard dogs in the cities, but the average visitor might never even see a Fila, though they are probably the most common dog in that country.

In the cities where crime is a major problem the property of many of the wealthier residents is surrounded by eight-foot-high cement walls. Writes Maggie Bob of the Fila Brasileiro Club of America, ". . . behind the walls of most middle- and upper middle-class houses in Rio de Janiero and

Champion Ojeriza's Battle Cry shares an affectionate moment with owner Linda Maggio.

São Paulo, that distant bark probably indicates that the family Fila is on guard duty."

Sometimes these dogs can be trained to accept the presence of a stranger if the owner is around. Quite often they simply have to be kenneled during the day, and allowed to roam behind the walls only at night when they are on guard duty.

A dog that aggressive is not suited to America where people live in houses with large, unfenced lawns, and casual visiting is part of everyday life.

It's the desire of responsible American Fila breeders to produce a Fila that is more in tune with life in modern

America. No one is trying to make a lap dog out of the Fila. The protectiveness and aggressiveness of the Fila is a major part of this dog's appeal. What U.S. breeders would like is a dog that is calm, stable, and highly trainable, a dog that will attack only when he or the people and property he is guarding are threatened. They certainly don't want dogs that may attack a judge in a show ring. That may be allowed in Brazil, but it would mean immediate disqualification in the United States.

Fortunately there are Filas in this country who do possess this ideal temperament. Responsible breeders are trying to make sure that this becomes standard for the breed. They are very worried that the Fila may find itself in the same sort of position as the Pit Bull—a dog with a reputation as a "killer"—and one that is banned in many communities.

"The atmosphere in the U.S. concerning protective dogs is grave and unsettling at this time," says the Fila Brasileiro Club of America newsletter. "We must produce dogs of stable temperament or our breed will, like the Pit Bull, be under fire from all quarters."

Unlike the Pit Bull, which has been used in illegal dog fights, the Fila is not a fighting dog. It is strictly a guard dog. At present there are only a few hundred of these dogs in the United States. They are very expensive, and hard to get. Most breeders are very well aware of the potential dangers of owning a Fila, even a stable, well-trained one. They want to sell their dogs only to those who are able to handle them properly.

The Fila is probably descended from the war dogs brought to the New World by the Portuguese and Spanish conquistadors. These in turn were descendants of the ferocious ancient Roman war dogs. Somewhere in the history of the

54

Fila a strain of hound, probably Bloodhound or Foxhound, was added to improve the dog's scenting abilities. Filas were used to hunt jaguars and wild boars, and to track down runaway slaves. In general, the Fila type was the large working dog of the sugar plantations and ranches of Brazil. There were no controlled breeding programs. No records were kept. The Fila didn't become a recognized breed in Brazil until 1946.

The modern Fila is a large, heavy-headed dog, with lots of loose skin around its head and neck—which may be due to its Bloodhound ancestry. This gives the Fila a "houndy" and deceptively friendly look. A large male will stand some thirty inches at the shoulder and weigh well over 100 pounds. They come in a variety of colors—practically anything but white and gray.

When walking, the Fila has a very fluid, almost catlike movement. It can gallop with incredible speed and agility for so large and heavy an animal. In the jungle the Fila's life depended on his speed, strength, and agility.

All in all, the Fila Brasileiro is a remarkable animal. But is such a dog suited for life in modern America? If its destiny is in the hands of responsible breeders and owners, the answer is yes.

Champion Greater Swiss Mountain Dogs, Connie and Bello

12. The Greater Swiss Mountain Dog

At one time wagons and carts were pulled by horses, donkeys, and in some parts of the world by large dogs. Then along came the railroad, cars, and trucks. These mechanical means of transportation were more efficient for hauling loads. So gradually the horse, donkey, and dog-drawn wagon and cart declined or disappeared. Since dog-drawn carts were much less common than those pulled by horses and donkeys, they disappeared most completely, and so did the dogs that pulled them—or very nearly disappeared.

Dog-drawn carts were particularly useful in certain parts of Europe where roads were narrow and steep. Cart-pulling dogs, or draft dogs, were used by gardeners, butchers, milkmen, bakers, and other small businessmen to move their wares. It was said that the large draft dogs were able to pull as much weight as a donkey. They were certainly easier to care for. The dogs could also be used to herd and protect livestock, and to guard the family.

Naturally, draft dogs would have to be large, heavy-bodied, and extremely strong to do their job. There was no regular or systematic breeding of these dogs. Generally each region had its own favorite.

The draft dogs of Switzerland were probably originally descended from the giant war dogs of the Roman legions. These were in turn descended from the ancient Tibetan Mastiff.

Among the cart dogs developed in Switzerland, the St. Bernard is certainly the best known. Its ancestors pulled carts as well as rescued travelers. Another is the Bernese Mountain Dog. These dogs were bred by the basket weavers of Berne, Switzerland, specifically for drawing their carts to market. Both the St. Bernard and the Bernese Mountain Dog are registered by the AKC in America.

Another dog from this same background that is just beginning to make its appearance in the United States is the Greater Swiss Mountain Dog. Most American fanciers of this dog call it the "Swissy" for short. In Europe it is sometimes referred to as the "*Grosse*" or greater.

Greater Swiss Mountain Dogs were used widely throughout Switzerland to pull carts and guard farms and herds for hundreds of years. By about 1900 it was believed that the type had become extinct. Then in 1908 a man named Franz

Schertenleib brought a large, strong, and relatively short-haired dog to a Swiss dog show. The animal caught the attention of Dr. Albert Heim, a Swiss geologist and dog lover who had a particular interest in saving the dogs of his native land. He recognized the animal, called Bello, as a marvelous example of a once-popular but now nearly extinct breed of cart dog. It was Heim who gave the breed the name Greater Swiss Mountain Dog or "Grosse Schweizer Sennenhund." He asked Swiss dog lovers to be on the lookout for other examples of this breed, in order to save it from extinction. A few were found and controlled breeding began. The breed was formally recognized by the Swiss Kennel Club in 1910. However, the Swissy did not reach America until 1968.

As you might assume, the Swissy is a large, heavily built

A Swissy named Merry-Go-Round's Constellation, better known as Connie

dog. It generally weighs between 120 and 140 pounds and stands about two feet tall at the shoulder. The coat is short with well-defined markings of black, white, and red.

American enthusiasts for this breed say that it makes the ideal family dog—though because of its size it's not really ideal for a small city apartment. The Swissy isn't a nervous or hyperactive dog, but because of its size it does need plenty of room to move around.

Its size alone makes the Swissy an excellent guard dog. They don't bark a great deal, but they will let you know when a stranger arrives. Their bark is deep and loud, and to those who don't know the dog, it is a frightening sound. They also have the reputation of being a dog that never sleeps, or at least one that sleeps very lightly. Every strange noise, every change in routine will find the Swissy up and attentive.

Yet the Swissy is not an attack dog; indeed, it's remarkably gentle. One Swissy owner, who also raised rabbits, found that the big dogs would often try to adopt the rabbits. They get along well with other dogs too.

Many Swissy owners buy or build carts for their dogs to pull. These dogs seem to take to being harnessed to a cart naturally, and will learn to pull them without much extra training. The Swissy is also a good dog for those who like strenuous backpacking. Just strap a pack to the dog's back and they are ready to go. They can even carry their own food.

A basketful of Havanese puppies

13. The Havanese

If little Shirley Temple, the tap dancing darling of old movies, had been born a dog she'd have been a Havanese. The Havanese is an adorable little animal, absolutely sparkling with star quality. It's one dog that can out-Poodle a Poodle. Playful clowns who once performed in traveling circuses, Havanese can be trained to climb ladders and jump through hoops. And they love to swim.

Some experts believe the Havanese come by their Poodle-like traits naturally because they're descended from Poodles.

Other experts say the Havanese is descended from the Maltese. Poodles everybody's seen and if you've ever been to an official AKC dog show you've also probably seen the small silky dog known as the Maltese. Another AKC-registered dog is a Bichon Frise. With its curly outer coat and plumy tail, the Bichon Frise is to the dog world what vanilla ice cream is to a sweet shop. Well, the Havanese is a member of the Bichon group of small long-haired dogs.

Toy-sized, the Havanese stands from eight to ten and one-half inches at the shoulder and generally weighs from seven to twelve pounds. The dog has a quick springy gait, carries its plumy tail high over its back, is long in body in proportion to its height, has long well-feathered ears, and soft beautiful dark eyes.

The Havanese coat is nonshedding and odorless and may be either wavy or curly. The straighter the coat, the less trimming required. Twice-a-week brushing is usually enough grooming for most Havanese pets. Show dogs, of course, require more. As for color, the Havanese coat comes in pretty shades of white, cream, chocolate, silver, gold, blue, black, champagne, or a combination of these colors. Champagne seems especially appropriate for the Havanese, since when they are puppies these dogs are tiny enough to fit into a champagne glass.

Do not, however, confuse small with frail. When it comes to stamina, good health, intelligence, and alertness, the Havanese stands ten feet tall. Being cute doesn't stop these small canines from being good watchdogs. Friendly to everyone as puppies, they tend to become wary of strangers once they grow up and always warn their owners by barking when someone is at the door. As far as their human family circle is concerned, they remain loyal and friendly all their lives.

A pair of Havanese

They're good at keeping each other company, too, and do well in bunches. Though short on inches, Havanese are strong on herding instincts. In their native Cuba they boldly kept the household chickens and turkeys from straying out of the barnyard and kept the family cow in line.

Although the dogs were so identified with Cuba that they were named after the island's largest city, no one seems to know just how they got to their Caribbean homeland in the first place. Many Cubans believe Italian sea captains brought the ancestors of the present-day Havanese to Cuba as gifts for the wives of rich Spanish sugar planters. The captains wanted to make a good impression on the powerful planters and what better way than to make a good impression on the planters' wives? The Havanese became the favorite pet of the wealthiest people in Cuba.

Everything went cheerfully along for the little long-haired dogs until the Cuban Revolution of the 1950s when the dogs' owners rushed to escape from Cuba. Only a few were able to bring their Havanese with them. But these few were enough, and through care, patience, and sound breeding practices, the dogs were not only saved but there are now several hundred of them. The Havanese have found a new home in America where they remain as charming as ever.

A pair of Jack Russell Terriers

14. The Jack Russell Terrier

Think hard! How many breeds of dogs do you know of named after a particular person? Yet there really was a man named Jack Russell. A highly colorful character, he was born in the late eighteenth century and so closely tied was he to the marvelous breed of terriers he developed and made famous that it would have been unthinkable to name the dogs anything but Jack Russell Terriers. No dog breeder has ever received a higher honor.

In Britain Jack Russell Terriers are sometimes called Parson Jack Russell Terriers. That's because Jack Russell was a parson in a very rural part of England. Not that Jack Russell fits our modern image of a clergyman. We tend to think of clergymen as spiritual or sensitive people. You'd probably have a clearer picture of what Jack Russell was really like if you picture him as a super jock. Tall and strong, he was crazy about wrestling and boxing. True to his time and place, most of all he loved to go fox hunting. He went hunting as often as he could for as long as he could. And he was absolutely devoted to the terriers he took fox hunting with him.

It was while Jack Russell was at college (Oxford) that he met a milkman with a female terrier named Trump. She was really something special and Jack Russell bought her from the milkman right then and there. It was thanks to Trump that he was able to launch one of the greatest breeding programs in canine history. In later years Jack Russell would hunt with no less a personage than Britain's Prince of Wales and the prince may actually have owned a portrait of the by then legendary Trump.

What made Jack Russell like Trump so much? To understand what he saw in her you have to know what a terrier was expected to do in a fox hunt in Russell's era. The word "terrier" stems from the Latin word "terra" meaning "earth." In a fox hunt a terrier was expected to "go to ground," literally forcing the fox out of its hole into the open. Once the fox was out of his hole, it was up to the quick-moving hounds and hunters on horseback to chase the animal.

Jack Russell himself described the ideal terrier by saying it should be shaped like an adult vixen (female fox). That meant that the dog should be about fourteen inches at the shoulders and weigh about fourteen pounds. Being shaped like a fox made it easier for a terrier to get inside the fox's underground hiding place. The dog should also be slim, well-balanced, athletic and strong, with long straight strong legs. A good terrier had to be a dog with stamina and endurance, able to run.

So now let's get back to Trump and what Jack Russell saw in her. First of all, she was mostly white in color. This was a distinct advantage because, though shaped like a fox, a white dog could never be confused with a fox (which is red) and perhaps be killed by mistake. Trump also had a thick, moderately wirey coat, which was just perfect for keeping out the rainy cold and dampness of the English climate. She had a good sense of smell, was very courageous, and was an eager worker. She was also known for her superior temperament and nothing was more important to Jack Russell in a terrier than temperament.

A timid dog was useless to him. The dog had to be brave enough and forward enough to force the fox out of its hole. But the dog wasn't supposed to hurt the fox. A fiercely aggressive or vicious terrier was a disaster in a fox hunt, since the dog might kill the fox while the fox was still in its underground hiding place.

Another reason why temperament was important to Jack Russell was because his dogs had to get along at least passably well with each other and with a pack of hounds. Jack Russell spent years perfecting the temperament of his dogs. The modern Wirehaired Fox Terrier is said to have evolved from the Jack Russell Terrier and in the early 1900s was the most popular dog in the world, mostly because of its wonderful temperament.

Because of his success in the world of dog breeding, Jack

Badger and Nettle, Jack Russell Terriers, with owner Paul Ross

Russell became one of the original founders of England's Kennel Club and in 1874 he judged Fox Terriers in the first sanctioned English Kennel Club show. But he preferred working dogs to show dogs and never had his own Jack Russell Terriers shown.

Jack Russell lived to the ripe old age of eighty-eight and died a hunter to the end, or so the story goes. When he was dying, his housekeeper heard soft and dim the sound of hunting calls coming from his room. She peeked in and found the old man feebly but eagerly hunting a flea on his bed, as if the flea were a fox. The old man was buried in his churchyard and a thousand people attended his funeral because they had loved him and had loved his dogs.

Certainly, there's no doubt about how deeply Jack Russell had loved his dogs. His study walls were covered with pictures of his favorite Terriers and he kept some with him at all times. He even had his armchairs upholstered in the hides of his deceased canines so he could be reminded of them at all times.

Nowadays most owners of Jack Russell Terriers don't take their dogs fox hunting. They're devoted to them because they make such handsome, loyal, and interesting pets.

Champion Little Lion Dog, Lowe-Ray's Cricket

15. The Little Lion Dog

If you think the only place you can see a lion is in a zoo, you're wrong. Try a rare breed dog show. Of course the lion you'll see at the zoo is a huge sandy-colored animal, while the lion you'll see at a rare breed dog show is an animal that stands eight to fifteen inches high at the shoulder and comes in a wide variety of beautiful colors. The leonine little canine can even be spotted. The one color the Little Lion Dog rarely is, however, is pure white. Despite their differences, it's no accident that the Little Lion Dog (also called

69

the Petit Chien Lion or Lowchen) was named after the king of beasts.

The reason is the dog's appearance. The fur of the Little Lion Dog's coat grows naturally in a pattern similar to the fur of a great big lion with a ruff about its head and shoulders. The way the Little Lion Dog's coat is clipped makes the resemblance even more striking. A thick mane is left around the dog's head and shoulders while the body is clipped but not shaved closely. The tail is clipped smooth with a plume, not a Poodle-like pompon, at the tip. The legs may be clipped with hair left at the ankles. The dog's coat should be harsh, never silky or over-manicured. This is definitely a sturdy rough-and-tumble kind of small dog and should look it.

Its resemblance to the magnificent lion isn't the only thing this interesting breed has going for itself. The Little Lion Dog is very intelligent, outgoing, friendly, moves with easy grace, is fearless, has a stable non-yappy sort of temperament, and generally gets along well with other dogs. It's small enough to live in an apartment, yet quite big enough in personality for any size house, is easy to take along in a car, and shows a lively curiosity in its surroundings. It can also look back on a very long history.

Centuries ago the breed developed in the Mediterranean regions of France, Italy, and Spain. Artists loved the look of the Little Lion Dog and you'll see the animal pictured in tapestries and paintings in many of Europe's finest museums. You'll find Little Lion Dogs in the fifteenth-century "Lady and the Unicorn" tapestries in the Cluny Museum in France, the pictures of the famous German artist Albrecht Durer (1471–1528), and the works of the great eighteenth-century Spanish painter Francisco de Goya. What's astonishing is how much the Little Lion Dog of today looks like its fifteenth-century and eighteenth-century ancestors.

Despite their proud history, by the beginning of the twentieth century Little Lion Dogs didn't seem to have much to look forward to. Scarcely anyone was interested in breeding them. The Second World War of the 1940s nearly spelled their doom. It is rumored that one of the last remaining breeders of the Little Lion Dog simply let his pets loose, desperately hoping they'd somehow survive on their own in war-torn Europe.

The breed was literally saved by one old woman who lived in Brussels, Belgium. She searched the streets of Brussels daily, taking in every Little Lion Dog she found. For twenty years she worked slowly and carefully to rebuild the breed. Next, interest in the Little Lion Dog surfaced in Germany. Then the British fell captive to the charms of the vigorous Little Lion Dog. Today the breed is very popular in England.

In America Bob and Carole Yhlen first heard of the Little Lion Dog in 1970. Both were intrigued by the idea of a dog that looked like a cat. Lions, the big roaring kind, had always fascinated Bob, maybe because he and Carole were both born in August under the sign of Leo in the Zodiac. Already pros at raising several breeds of AKC-registered dogs, they decided to devote themselves instead to introducing the Little Lion Dog to America. The first Little Lion Dogs were imported to the United States in 1971 and a small enthusiastic band of dog lovers joined the Yhlens in working toward the goal of bringing the breed to its fullest potential. The Little Lion Dog Club of America was formed, with a newsletter cleverly called *Headlions,* and a breed registry was created. The club is committed to achieving AKC recognition someday.

As far as the Yhlens are concerned, things do get a little wacky at times. Take the day Bob was invited to a charitable fund raiser along with other owners of unusual breeds of dogs. The dogs were at the fund raiser, too, of course. But they weren't expected to appear in costume. The owners were. The owner's costume was supposed to remind people of the country the dogs originally came from. Bob chose France to represent one of the Little Lion Dog's native lands. And how did six-foot-three Bob Yhlen dress for the occasion? Why, he went as the early nineteenth-century French hero Napoleon who was only five-foot-two. There stood very tall Bob in tricornered hat, tights, and gold-braided coat, surrounded by Little Lion Dogs, all the while asking himself how he could possibly be doing such a completely goofy thing.

Bob also owns and operates an electronic design and manufacturing business and new customers are usually startled to find half a dozen Little Lion Dogs running around Bob's office. After all, people don't usually take their dogs to work. But that's the depth of love and loyalty Little Lion Dogs inspire in their breeders and owners.

Neapolitan Mastiff, Del Querceto Brutus

16. The Neapolitan Mastiff

Once you see a Neapolitan Mastiff you are not likely to forget it. The "Neo," as it is popularly called, is huge—a full-grown male can weigh well over 150 pounds, and 200-pounders are not unknown. The broad head has an abundance of folds and wrinkles, and the massive muscular body looks powerful, and is. Usually the Neo moves with a lumbering, bearlike gait, but it can be alarmingly quick and agile. The Neo doesn't look like the sort of dog anyone would challenge.

Yet despite its intimidating size and appearance, the Neapolitan Mastiff is not a ferocious or aggressive dog. Of course, it wouldn't be wise to go charging, unannounced, into a yard guarded by one of these giants. It's not a good idea to go charging unannounced into a yard guarded by any large dog—or by most small dogs, for that matter. The Neo can be very protective of its own territory, but it's not looking for a fight.

Many authorities believe that the ancestors of these dogs were first brought from Asia to Greece by the soldiers of Alexander the Great, about 300 B.C. From Greece they were taken to Italy. Among the Greeks, large dogs were often used by soldiers in battle, and the practice seems to have spread to the armies of Rome.

The Roman war dogs were called the Mollusers, and they are believed to be the direct ancestors of a number of modern breeds, though statues and drawings show that they most closely resemble the Neapolitan Mastiff. In battle the Mollusers would wear a spiked collar and often padded armor. They could be used to attack foot soldiers or horses, causing them to throw their riders. These ferocious Roman war dogs were much feared.

Naturally, the Romans, who delighted in bloodthirsty gladiatorial fights and wild animal fights, also used the huge dogs in the arena. However, they appear to have been most highly valued as guard dogs.

Columella, a Roman writer of the first century, described the ideal guard dog of that era:

"The guard dog for the house should be black (or dark) so that during the day, when he is seen by a thief, his appearance will be frightening. When night falls, the dog, lost in the shadows, can attack without being seen. Its head is so massive that it seems to be the most important part of the body. The ears fall toward the front, the brilliant and penetrating eyes are black or gray. The chest is deep and hairy . . ."

A fearsome appearance was considered a great asset of these dogs. Five hundred years after Columella, another writer, the Italian naturalist Aldrovandus, said that this dog ". . . should be a terrifying aspect and look as though he was going to fight and be an enemy to everybody except his master; so much so that he will not allow himself to be stroked even by those he knows best, but threatens everybody alike by showing his teeth and always looks at everybody as though he was burning with anger and glares around in every direction with a hostile glance."

A terrifying animal indeed!

In 1897 an Italian veterinarian wrote a popular book on dogs. He said that this Mastiff was particularly useful in the city of Naples where there were many thieves. The veterinarian also said that this dog was so strong it was able to take on an angry bull. The Neo would grab the bull's mouth in its own jaws, and hold on until the bull realized who was boss, and calmed down.

"He [the Neo] is high-spirited with children and small dogs. It's not in his character to pick a fight without reason. But if provoked, watch out. This dog will not overlook an affront to its dignity."

The Neo continued to be used as a guard dog on estates, mostly in southern Italy, remaining relatively unknown elsewhere. Oddly it wasn't until the dark days of World War II, when a lot of breeds of dogs in Europe nearly became extinct, that this breed's popularity began to grow. Perhaps it was the hardships of war that made the people of Italy look for ways to express their national pride. It was in 1942, with bombs quite literally falling all around, that the first standard for the Neapolitan Mastiff was drawn up, and these huge animals began appearing in the dog show rings for the first time.

In Italy the strength of the breed has become almost legendary. Lots of stories, many of them probably exaggerated ones, are told about it. A dog that figures in many of these tales was a huge, dark gray beast called Masaniello. One account tells of two men trying to push a small truck out of a hole in the middle of a road. They pushed with all their might, but couldn't budge the truck. Standing at the side of the road watching this was a small round man accompanied by a large gray dog. Every time the truck slipped back into the hole the little man laughed. Finally, the truck

Del Querceto Brutus

owner and his friend became so exasperated that they went up to the little man and said, "If you think this so funny, see what you can do."

Without a word the little man took a heavy rope, tied one end to the truck's front bumper and the other to his dog's collar.

"Pull, Masaniello," he said quietly. The big dog pulled, and slowly the truck began to move. Its front wheel cleared the hole. Then, without saying anything else, the little man untied his dog and walked away. He was smiling.

One day Masaniello's owner took him to the vet. He and the dog were sitting in the waiting room when some of the owner's friends came by. They figured that the famous dog was getting old and weak, and they said so.

Masaniello's owner pointed to one of the benches in the waiting room, which happened to be bolted to the floor. He said to the dog, "Your master would like to take this home." The Mastiff gripped the bench in his jaws and ripped it from the floor. No one spoke about Masaniello getting old and weak anymore.

A traveler walking near the city of Pompeii, in southern Italy, stopped to rest and eat his lunch under some fig trees. Suddenly he heard a low rumbling sound behind him, and he turned to find himself looking directly into the enormous, wrinkled face of a gray Neo. The dog came over and placed its head firmly on the traveler's shoulder. The terrified man didn't know what to do, but after a moment he reached up and scratched the dog's ears and head, which the huge beast seemed to enjoy. The trouble was that the man was afraid to stop, and the scratching went on for over an hour.

Finally, the dog's master came by. "Oh, don't worry about

him," the man said. "It's daytime and he's very friendly. He guards these fields, but he works only at night. If you came back in the dark he would give you a very different welcome."

In Italy a good Neo is extremely expensive and difficult to obtain. Old-time breeders are often reluctant to sell good dogs to people they don't know. Some Neos were brought to this country by people of Italian descent, who had seen the dog when they were children in Italy, and had never forgotten it, or who had heard about the legendary dog from their parents or grandparents.

In the United States and Canada the Neo is still rare, and commands very high prices. It's not a nervous or hyperactive dog, but because of its sheer size and bulk, it can't be kept in confined spaces. Still, the popularity of this ancient breed is very definitely on the rise.

Nova Scotia Duck Tolling Retrievers, Val and Rusty

17. The Nova Scotia Duck Tolling Retriever

This dog has a long and funny-sounding name. The Nova
Scotia part refers to the eastern province of Canada where
this particular breed was developed. "Duck" simply means
that it was used by duck hunters. There are a whole variety
of hunting dogs called retrievers, whose task it is to pick
up and bring back what the hunter has shot. It's the "tolling"
part of the name that confuses most people. What is tolling?

A tolling dog will run up and down along the shoreline
and attract the attention of curious ducks, who will swim
or fly in as much as a mile just to see what's going on.

As is usual in the early history of dogs, no one actually knows where the idea of tolling dogs began. Some say it began in England, but most Canadians insist that it is a practice that developed first in Canada. Some hunters have observed foxes running up and down along the shore wagging their bushy tails. When an overcurious duck got too close it was grabbed either by the agile fox or its mate, who had been hiding along the shore. This was called tolling. Somewhere, either in England or Canada, hunters began to train dogs to imitate the foxes' tolling activity. Some believe that the Indians of Canada's Micmac tribe were the first to develop tolling dogs, though this is far from certain.

What is known is that Nova Scotia hunters began deliberately to develop toller-type dogs as early as the mid-1890s, and by the turn of the century a dog called the Yarmouth or Little River Toller was well known by hunters not only in Canada but well down the East Coast of the United States.

The modern Nova Scotia Duck Tolling Retriever probably is a mix of many other breeds—the general Labrador type, a Brown Spaniel, Collies, Chesapeakes, perhaps even Beagles or Springer Spaniels.

The result is a handsome reddish-brown dog that looks remarkably like a fox. This has led to the myth that the Toller is really descended from crosses between foxes and dogs. Scientists, however, insist that such crosses are highly unlikely—and that the Toller is simply a dog that looks, and occasionally acts, like a fox, rather than a fox-dog crossbreed.

The modern Toller is trained to work with the hunter. The hunter hides in his blind by the lake shore. He tosses out a ball or a stick that the dog enthusiastically picks up and brings back to the blind. Time and time again the hunter tosses out the stick or ball, and time and time again the dog leaps out after it, wagging its tail and apparently paying no attention to the ducks at all. Some species of ducks seem to be attracted by this sort of activity, while others pay no attention, and some ducks are actually alarmed and fly away.

However, this type of hunting has become less popular in recent years—probably because of the general decline in

Rusty, a Tolling Retriever

the number of ducks and the increased use of motorboats by hunters. The Toller has been used more and more as an ordinary Retriever. In fact, by the 1940s, the Toller was in danger of vanishing as a separate breed. Then a few dedicated devotees of this dog began keeping accurate breeding records, and began breeding programs. The breed began to rebound.

Today, Tollers can be found in many parts of the world, and while there are only a few hundred registered Tollers at any one time, their existence is no longer threatened.

Indeed, the Toller may be taking on an entirely new career, not as a hunter but as a pet or companion dog. Many of today's most common pet dogs, like the Cocker Spaniel and Beagle, originally began as hunting dogs.

In many ways the Toller is an ideal family pet. They are medium-sized dogs; the males stand twenty inches at the shoulder and weigh around fifty pounds. Females are a bit smaller. Tollers are easily trainable, and it's their natural playfulness that made them a distinct breed in the first place.

While the Nova Scotia Duck Tolling Retriever is not yet a registered AKC breed in the United States, it has been registered with the Canadian Kennel Club since 1945. Indeed, some Toller fanciers say that this animal is not only *a* Canadian Dog, but *the* Canadian dog. *Vancouver Sun* columnist Lee Straight has written that it is the only truly Canadian breed. "The Labrador and Newfoundland may have been started here but were perfected in Britain." The Toller, said Straight, is truly unique to Canada.

Coated Peruvian Inca Orchid. There is also a Hairless variety.

18. The Peruvian Inca Orchid

No breed of dog in the world has as exotic and beautiful a name as the Peruvian Inca Orchid. How many dogs, after all, are named after a flower?

The hairless variety of the Peruvian Inca Orchid is quite colorful. Though no particular color is preferred, the dogs are usually pink or white with splotches of color splashed on their smooth soft skin. They've been known to turn a redder shade of pink when upset, reminding their owners of a blushing human being.

The furry variety of the Peruvian Inca Orchid is usually white with here and there a large spot of color. Under the coat the dog's skin may be mottled, just like the hairless variety. As for the coat itself, it can be short or fairly long, and it may sometimes be slightly curly.

It is said that the dogs were highly valued by the Incas, Indians who ruled over a vast and fascinating civilization in ancient Peru. Unlike other breeds with a heavy strain of hairlessness, these animals are hounds, sight hounds to be exact, that is, dogs that hunt by sight rather than smell. Like other sight hounds (Borzois, for example), Peruvian Inca Orchids are trim, fast, and graceful. Medium-sized, the males stand seventeen to twenty inches at the shoulder. Sweetly tempered, the dogs respond well to gentle treatment, and owners quickly become extremely fond of these quiet and loyal canines.

There are only a small number of Peruvian Inca Orchids around. Here in the United States, at least, they are among the rarest of rare breeds.

The original Peruvian Inca Orchid was probably furred, with the hairless variety appearing later as a mutation (an instant genetic change). Dogs with hair and dogs without hair can be born in the same litter. The hairless dogs will grow to maturity without a full set of teeth. The furry Peruvian Inca Orchid usually has a full set of teeth. Smart breeders know that the progress and health of the entire breed rests on making the right use of the coated variety in any breeding program.

One of the big differences between the two varieties of Peruvian Inca Orchid is the ears. Hairless dogs have upright ears which they can fold back. Add fur, and the weight of the fur on the ears causes the ears to drop. Whatever the ears and whether furry or furless, Peruvian Inca Orchids should always have almond-shaped eyes brimming with intelligence and alertness, light but strong bones, good muscles, and powerful hind legs. This is certainly no everyday ordinary garden variety of dog.

A young Petit Basset Griffon Vendeen

19. The Petit Basset Griffon Vendeen

This small French scent hound (a dog that hunts mainly by scent or smell) has a very big name, but each part of the name helps describe the dog. "Petit" means small. "Basset" lets you know that the dog has short legs and is low to the ground. "Griffon" describes its coat and means wirehaired. "Vendeen" refers to the rugged Vendee province of France where the animal comes from. Called "the happy breed" because of its engaging personality, this great-looking dog also goes by a variety of different nicknames. In England it's Roughie. In Denmark it's Griffon. In the United States it's either Petit or the neatly rhyming PBGV.

The PBGV stands thirteen to fifteen inches at the shoulder. Small, yes, but tiny, no. The reason there's a Petit in its name is to distinguish it from its slightly larger relative, the Grand (Big) Basset Griffon Vendeen. Petits were used to hunt rabbits, Grands to hunt small deer and wolves. Grands and Petits were interbred until the mid-1970s and both were often found in the same litter. Interbreeding is no longer allowed.

It was in 1983 that the PBGV really grabbed the dog world by the tail. That's when a twelve-week-old Canadian Petit puppy took Best Puppy in Show at the Professional Handler's Association Super Match Show in New Jersey. The precious pup got tons of attention and many dog lovers in the United States were suddenly fascinated by a breed they'd never heard of before.

That dog fanciers liked what they saw is understandable. The PBGV has large dark eyes, heavy eyebrows, ears that reach almost to the end of its nose, a beard, and moustache. It carries its slim medium-length tail proudly. It has a long rough coat and a thick undercoat. Though the coat needs brushing, it should never be trimmed. The dog shouldn't even be bathed very often because baths soften its fur. The PBGV's low-slung body is muscular. It comes in white with lemon, orange, tricolor, or grizzle markings.

The PBGV is supposed to be a rustic-looking hound. That means it should look natural, outdoorsy. It's a doggy sort of dog. There's a reason for the low body, the rough fur, the dog's overall appearance. The landscape of the dog's native Vendee is harsh, a tangled mass of plants and thorny shrubs. Hunting in Vendee is very difficult. Horses can't get

Petit Basset Griffon Vendeen

through. A smooth-coated dog would injure its skin crossing the terrain. PBGVs are built for moving comfortably through just such a challenging region.

A small number of PBGVs were imported to the United States in the early 1970s to form a pack of hunting hounds in Pennsylvania. These days most PBGVs, at least on this side of the Atlantic Ocean, are either show dogs or pets. The breed was recognized by the Canadian Kennel Club in 1985 and many breeders and owners in the United States are hoping for AKC recognition someday.

Despite the low-slung shape, don't confuse the PBGV with the Basset Hound. Basset Hounds are easy-going, low-key canines. The PBGV is full of energy. In some ways it's more like a terrier than a hound. Outgoing, friendly, but definitely independent, a PBGV is a dog with a mind of its own. The dog enjoys attention but will not beg for it.

Boredom is a word that doesn't exist in a PBGV's vocabulary. The dog is loaded with curiosity and enjoys exploring the world. If given half a chance it will go off after an interesting smell. So if you own a PBGV you have to make sure it's either on leash or in a safely enclosed yard when it's out of the house. That's not as easy as it sounds because this alert, athletic, and highly self-confident canine can dig its way under or jump over many a fence.

Since the PBGV originally hunted in packs, it can live comfortably with other canines. As for being a watchdog, it will certainly let you know when anyone approaches the house. Actually, it will let you know a lot of things. A PBGV likes to use its nice hound-sounding voice. It is not a quiet dog.

Does the Petit Basset Griffon Vendeen deserve to be called "the happy breed?" You bet it does. If you meet one, just take a look at its tail. You'll find that a PBGV's tail is almost always wagging.

Vladek and Krymka are Polish Lowland Sheepdogs, better known as PONS.

20. The PONS (Polish Lowland Sheepdog)

Polka bands and polka dancers weren't the only star acts at the 1983 Polish-American Festival in Baltimore, Maryland. A small cluster of wonderfully furry dogs held center stage. They were Polish Lowland Sheepdogs. Well, their official name is really Polski Owczarek Nizinny, but everybody calls them PONS, from the initials in their name.

A Bearded Collie breeder imported the first PONS to America in the 1970s, but the people who really put the PONS on the map in this country were Kazmir and Betty

Augustowski of Maryland. It was thanks to the Augustowskis that the crowd-pleasing PONS were at Baltimore's Polish-American Festival. Old hands at raising dogs, the Augustowskis had bred Shih Tzus, Dachshunds, and Maltese for years before they became interested in PONS. Proud of their Polish heritage, they were eager to see a breed of dogs from Poland become established in the United States. Establishing a Polish breed here turned out to be anything but easy.

Through an ad in a dog magazine Betty learned that someone in New York had imported a pair of PONS from Warsaw, Poland's major city. The pair of PONS had produced a litter of pups. One pup was left for sale. Delighted, the Augustowskis bought it. The person who sold them the puppy was a PONS fan, but had no further plans for importing or breeding the Polish dogs. The next move was up to the Augustowskis. That was in 1982.

The Augustowskis began their search for more PONS. At first it was a frustrating search. They contacted the very few people in America who owned the dog. No luck. They wrote rare breed clubs. Nothing happened. They got in touch with breeders in Poland and even asked the Polish Consul in New York to help them. When nothing worked they went to Poland. In the end their efforts paid off.

A Polish breeder sent the Augustowskis a female named Krymka, who had a litter of puppies a few weeks after she arrived in America. Both Krymka and the father of her pups were registered with the Polish Kennel Club. Not only that, the father was an important champion. Instantly the Augustowskis started promoting and publicizing the appealing PONS. Soon they were joined by a small group of devoted PONS fanciers who were also interested in breeding the dogs. The PONS were in America to stay.

The PONS is a medium-sized dog standing seventeen to twenty inches at the shoulder, small for a European herding dog. You'll find the PONS mainly on farms in Poland where they've herded sheep and cattle for centuries. No PONS can become a champion in its homeland until it has first earned a working certificate, that is, proven its skill as a herding dog.

Despite its value to Polish farmers, the PONS was practically extinct by the end of World War II. It wasn't that people lost interest in the breed. The reason the PONS almost disappeared was because life was so hard in Poland during the war that people had to worry about people, not dogs. It took a Polish veterinarian fifteen years to rebuild the breed after World War II ended in 1945.

Twenty years later the PONS was ready to make its post-war dog show debut. That year nine PONS were entered in the World Show in Berne, Switzerland. They all did fabulously well. To show you just how much the PONS has progressed since then, at the 1985 dog show in Poznan, Poland, there were fifty-nine PONS entered.

Somewhere in the PONS background may be the Puli, a dog with a thick corded coat. If you've ever seen a Puli at an AKC dog show you know it looks like a dog totally encased in a braided blanket. Obviously the PONS has other dogs in its background because it doesn't look like that. The PONS does look somewhat like a Bearded Collie, another dog you may have seen at an AKC dog show. There is a theory that Polish sailors trading with Scotland brought the PONS to the Scottish coast where the PONS was bred to Scottish herding dogs. The result? The Bearded Collie.

Though the PONS is a hard worker, it also makes a super pet. A pet PONS is easily trained, handles children gently, loves its family, and gets along well with other animals. Aloof with strangers, the PONS can also do the job of protecting its home and owners. In America PONS are used as therapy dogs, visiting sick and homebound people to cheer them up. Some PONS work on dude ranches, rounding up horses.

Part of the charm of a PONS is its looks. Covered with shaggy hair, it has a medium-sized head that looks much larger, thanks to all the fur on its forehead, cheeks, and chin. Sharp eyes peek out at you from the mass of hair or else are hidden by it. What you do notice about a PONS is its big blunt nose. A PONS has a solid muscular body, and a nice ambling sort of walk. A wide range of colors and markings are permitted, but the dog is usually white with patches of black, gray, sandy gray, sandy beige, or russet.

You do have to brush and groom a PONS. But so what? In the world of canines nothing's more fun than a really shaggy dog.

Puffin Dog puppies, five weeks old

21. The Puffin Dog

If ever there was a dog designed for mountain climbing it's the Puffin Dog, which comes from Norway, a country famous for its mountains. Most dogs have four toes that touch the ground and a dewclaw way above the other toes that doesn't reach the ground when a dog walks. You can think of a dewclaw as a kind of false toe. The Puffin Dog is different. It has six toes. Five are regular toes, the sixth is the dewclaw. Having an extra toe on each paw comes in very handy going uphill. It helps the Puffin Dog keep its balance climbing even the sheerest of cliffs.

There are other oddities about the Puffin Dog. Like a reindeer, a Puffin Dog can turn its neck so far backwards it can touch its spine with its nose. It can fold down its ears and close them tight against snow, rain, and dirt. The dogs have amazingly flexible shoulders. They even walk funny, moving with a kind of paddling motion. Again, it's a way of walking best meant for mountain climbing, not for meandering across a flat field.

You'd expect a mountain-climbing dog to appeal to a mountain-climbing human. So when British-born mountain climber Paul Ross, who runs a mountain-climbing school in Conway, New Hampshire, first learned there was such a creature as a Puffin Dog it's hardly surprising that he began dreaming about importing the breed to America. Rare breeds of dogs were nothing new to Ross, who is one of the foremost Jack Russell Terrier breeders in the world. He soon found out that getting a Puffin Dog out of Norway wasn't going to be easy. To understand why, we must first take a closer look at that funny name "Puffin Dog." Puffins are seabirds and for centuries Puffin Dogs were bred on two remote islands solely to hunt them. The coastal cliffs of Norway were once filled with puffins and because they roosted high atop the cliffs above the sea they were hard to catch. Yet Norwegian farmers relied on them as a source of food and added to their incomes by selling the birds' feathers.

With their remarkable six-toed feet, Puffin Dogs could reach the cliff tops where the seabirds roosted. Thanks to their flexible shoulders, they could scrunch themselves up and crawl into the narrow cracks and clefts where the seabirds laid their eggs. Because they could touch their spines with their noses, they were able to get in and out of the tightest spots and turn around just about anywhere. When

95

they sought the birds in mountain caves, they could shut their ear drums to keep out the dirt and wet.

For a variety of reasons the puffin has become rarer and rarer in Norway and today the bird is strictly protected there. The Puffin Dog doesn't hunt the puffin bird anymore. As has happened with so many other breeds over the years, the Puffin Dog went into decline and by 1943 there were only about sixty Puffin Dogs left in all of Norway. That was bad enough, but just as they were making a comeback a terrible outbreak of distemper practically wiped out the breed. By 1962 fewer than ten were left. Devoted breeders gave their all and managed to save the Puffin Dog from extinction, but even now there are only a few hundred Puffin Dogs in Norway and breeders will not sell their dogs to just anybody who happens to want one. It took effort, persistence, luck,

Female Puffin Dog

and skill for Paul Ross to acquire the very first Puffin Dog ever sent to America.

A Norwegian Puffin Club of America has been established and the club works closely with expert Norwegian breeders. The club is committed to encouraging serious responsible dog breeders and doesn't want to sell the dogs simply as pets. It's going to be hard enough developing this exceptional breed in America, even through the work of the most devoted breeders. That's because the Puffin Dog has very small litters. Females give birth to no more than two or three pups at a time.

There are lots of good reasons for cheering on this small breed besides its talent for climbing mountains. Puffin Dogs are friendly. They get along not only with people and each other but with many different breeds of dogs. They're active and love to take long walks.

Despite being named after a bird (by the way, in Norwegian the word for puffin is *Lunde* and these dogs are sometimes called Lundehunds), the Puffin Dog looks a lot like a fox. Basically small animals, males stand thirteen to fourteen or so inches at the shoulder. Females are slightly smaller. The dogs generally weigh thirteen to fifteen pounds. Mostly they're an attractive shade of brown with white markings around the neck and on the lower legs, but sometimes they come in two other colors, black or white. Their coats are dense and they have light brown eyes.

The Puffin Dog still has an uphill climb ahead of it before it becomes a familiar face in America. But then, conquering mountains is what this breed is all about.

Litter of Shar-Pei puppies from Corrugated Shar-Pei. Sire is Champion Norman T. Foo of D.J.'s Shar-Pei. Dam is Corrugated Annie.

22. The Shar-Pei

In the 1960s the Chinese Shar-Pei was listed in the *Guinness Book of World Records* as the rarest dog in the world. Its numbers had declined so alarmingly that it seemed doomed to extinction as a distinct breed within a very few years.

Today the Shar-Pei is "rare" only because the breed has not been fully recognized by the American Kennel Club. It is certainly the best known of the rare breeds. The reason for this astonishing turn-around can be summed up in one word—*wrinkles*. The Shar-Pei, particularly as a puppy, has more wrinkles than any other dog in the world. This makes it not only distinctive, but irresistibly cute.

The Shar-Pei is not a new breed. Its history can be traced back nearly two thousand years. And don't let that cute look fool you—the Shar-Pei was never bred to be an ornament or a lap dog.

The Shar-Pei was developed in China. Statues of Shar-Pei-like dogs have been found in ancient Chinese tombs. In fact, so many statues were found that the animals were sometimes referred to as Tomb Dogs.

The ancestors of the modern Shar-Pei were probably a good deal larger than the breed we know today. They were originally working dogs. Peasants and farmers used them for herding and protection.

They were also used as fighting dogs. At one time dog fighting was a popular "sport" in China, as it was in many other countries in the world. Gamblers would bet on the fights. Even today the Shar-Pei is sometimes referred to as the Chinese Fighting Dog.

Some of the Shar-Pei's physical characteristics may give it an edge in fighting. The name Shar-Pei means "sand skin." The dog's coat is extremely rough and bristly. It's not the sort of coat another dog would like to get hold of. The abundance of loose and wrinkled skin is another advantage. That would allow the dog to fight back even while being held. All that skin would help to protect vital internal organs from injury. The small deep-set eyes and tiny ears gave the opponent little to get hold of. The Shar-Pei also has good strong jaws and a large mouth.

While the Chinese undoubtedly did use the Shar-Pei for fighting, its reputation as a fighter may have been exaggerated. Unlike some dogs that have been specially bred for fighting, the Shar-Pei isn't all that aggressive. It might have been built to fight, but it didn't really like to fight. It was generally replaced by larger and more aggressive Western breeds in dog fighting in China. The Shar-Pei then went back to being what it had always primarily been, a companion and protector of farm and family.

The crisis for the Shar-Pei, and for many other Chinese breeds, began during the hardships of World War II and the victory of the Communist Party in China. Faced with a large and largely underfed human population, the Communist leaders decided that dogs were a luxury China simply could not afford. By the late 1940s there were very few dogs left in China. The Shar-Pei, which had been a dog of the poverty-stricken peasant, virtually disappeared in its native land.

However, some Shar-Peis survived in Hong Kong, a Chinese city that was ruled by the British. A man named Matgo Law, who owned Shar-Peis in Hong Kong, feared that one day China might take over Hong Kong and the breed would then become completely extinct. The only way to prevent this was to have people in other countries a long way from China take an interest in the breed.

Law wrote to an American magazine about the dog, asking American dog lovers to help save the breed. He also enclosed a number of Shar-Pei photographs. He didn't know what kind of response he would get. Indeed, he didn't know if he would get any response at all. He soon discovered that the Shar-Pei had a lot of potential friends in America. Over two hundred people wrote to Law, asking where they could get Shar-Pei puppies. There weren't enough Shar-Peis in Hong Kong to fill all the orders.

Slowly a few Shar-Peis began to make their way into the United States. The more Americans saw of these very unique

100

Champion Shar-Pei, Norman T. Foo

dogs, the more they loved them. Pictures of Shar-Peis, particularly the heavily wrinkled puppies, began appearing first in magazines for dog breeders, then in popular magazines for the general public. Shar-Peis began showing up on television programs like "Good Morning, America," and the "Tonight Show." In a very short time, or so it seemed, what had once been billed as the rarest dog in the world was appearing everywhere. Currently Shar-Peis are among the most popular dog "models" used in advertising. Even if you have never seen one "in person" you have certainly seen pictures of a Shar-Pei and seen them on TV.

The driving force behind this publicity blitz is Ernest and Madeline Albright of California. They were among the first Americans to get Shar-Peis from Hong Kong. They began a deliberate campaign to publicize and popularize the dog. And the campaign has certainly succeeded. Not only has the Shar-Pei become well known, its numbers have mushroomed. From being the "rarest dog in the world," there are now over 15,000 Shar-Peis registered in the United States alone, and that number is growing daily.

At dog shows which feature rare breeds, there are generally more Shar-Peis than any other breed. The Shar-Pei is not officially recognized by the American Kennel Club yet, but Shar-Pei breeders are working hard to have their breed part of the AKC.

Not all dog breeders believe that it is a good idea for a breed to become so popular so quickly. Any breed which suddenly experiences the sort of explosion of numbers that has been seen in the Shar-Pei faces many problems. There is no time to breed selectively, using only the best and healthiest representatives of the breed. The dogs are still very expensive, and the profit that can be made on them attracts unscrupulous breeders. Anyone thinking of buying a Shar-Pei must be careful to choose a reputable breeder. And the Shar-Pei's potential health problems should be discussed, fully and frankly.

With all its folds and wrinkles the Shar-Pei puppy is one of the cutest creatures on earth. When it grows up, however, while it certainly does not lose its wrinkles, they are less prominent. The adult Shar-Pei is really handsome rather than just cute. It's a medium-sized dog, weighing between thirty-five and sixty pounds. They are muscular dogs, and come in a wide variety of colors from pale cream to solid black. Like all dogs, the Shar-Pei needs exercise, but it is not an overly active breed, and is well suited for the rather confined conditions of modern life.

Despite its "fighting dog" ancestry, the Shar-Pei is quite friendly, particularly to members of "its family." As adults, they can be aloof with strangers, but never vicious or aggressive.

In short, the Shar-Pei makes an excellent pet and companion. It seems destined to rise from being the world's rarest dog to one of the world's best-known and best-loved. There is no greater success story in all modern dogdom.

There was a blue ribbon for this Shiba.

23. The Shiba

The Japanese are proud of their history and their traditions. They work very hard to preserve things they consider purely Japanese. Artwork, buildings, even people can be declared precious national products by the government. These treasures are to be revered and protected. Dogs, too, can be declared national treasures of Japan. In 1936 a native Japanese dog called the Shiba was given this official recognition.

No one really knows where or when the breed we now

call the Shiba or Shiba Inu began. Its ancestors came from mountainous regions and were used primarily for hunting. The ancient Shiba was larger and heavier than the modern dog.

For centuries Japan had deliberately isolated itself from the outside world. Then in 1854 this policy of isolation was changed. As a result, a lot of foreigners came to Japan, and many brought their dogs with them. To the Japanese these foreign breeds were exotic and became very popular. Many interbred with the native dogs, and some native Japanese breeds simply disappeared. The Shiba, which lived mainly in the isolated mountain regions, remained relatively untouched. It, too, might have disappeared had it not been for the special protection given to it in 1936.

Even so, the Shiba and other native Japanese breeds nearly became extinct during World War II. A small number survived, and today the Shiba is once again extremely popular throughout Japan. Aside from national pride, there are practical reasons for the Shiba's popularity in its native land. Japan is a very crowded country. Though the Japanese people love dogs, most simply don't have the space to keep a large dog. Very small dogs—usually called toy dogs—are most popular in Japan. The Shibas aren't toy-sized—they average about fifteen inches in height at the shoulder and weigh around forty-five pounds—but they are among the smaller native Japanese breeds. They can fit into the crowded life-style of modern Japan.

The Shiba first came to America after World War II. It was brought here by Army families that had been stationed in Japan and fell in love with the breed. It wasn't until 1979 that a litter of Shibas was actually born in the United States. The breeder was Julia Caldwell of California.

Her introduction to the Shiba was entirely accidental. One day she found an unusual-looking red dog wandering along a busy freeway during rush hour. The dog seemed lost and confused. She managed to coax the dog into her car and take it home with her. Inevitably Mrs. Caldwell's children called the dog "Rusty" because of his reddish coat and foxy look. Since Rusty didn't look like any dog Mrs. Caldwell had ever seen before, she did a little research. In a library book she saw a picture of a Shiba and it looked just like the dog she had found. She contacted the Japanese Consulate in San Francisco for more information, but they told her that there were no Shibas in the United States as far as they knew.

Mrs. Caldwell, who was not easily discouraged, finally wrote to the Japanese Kennel Club, enclosing a picture of Rusty. It was then she discovered that the Japanese take the Shiba's status as a national treasure very seriously. The Japanese Kennel Club actually sent one of its members to America to evaluate Rusty. He was declared a purebred Shiba, and Mrs. Caldwell was sent official papers for the dog. After further negotiations she was able to obtain a mate for Rusty from Japan.

The Shiba is one of those rare breeds which seems destined for ever-expanding popularity in the United States. They are small, active, and alert, thus well suited for life in the city, suburbs, or country. Remember that they are popular pets even in the crowded cities of Japan. They make excellent watchdogs. They will bark at strangers, but they don't bark all the time. They are suspicious of other dogs, but not particularly aggressive toward them. The Shiba will get along fine with other dogs, particularly if it has been raised with them.

The Shiba is quick, almost catlike in its motions. It's a tremendous jumper, and will sometimes leap high in the air in an attempt to catch birds. It will also catch rats and mice.This is doubtless part of its ancient heritage as a hunter of small game.

The Shiba is a very clean dog, sometimes engaging in the catlike activity of washing its face with its front paws. Some observers have said that the Shiba is really a cat in a dog costume—but that's not so. The Shiba is all dog.

The Shiba's pointy nose, pointy ears, and curled tail give it the look of a miniature sled dog. It is probably related—distantly—to such dogs as the Husky and the Samoyed. The Shiba is certainly related to the Akita, a massive Japanese guard dog, which has attained both popularity and AKC recognition in the United States.

The Shiba is a natural dog—that is, it requires no special trimming or other care. It comes in a variety of colors with red probably being the most popular. It has a double coat—a soft wooly undercoat which provides insulation, for the Shiba is an all-weather dog, and a harsh straight outer coat which protects against dirt and water. The Shiba sheds—a lot. The National Shiba Club of America warns that if you, or anyone in your family has an allergy to animal hair then this is not the dog for you. And on their list of "Don'ts" the club says, "Don't buy a Shiba if you don't enjoy vacuuming hair."

So while the Shiba makes an excellent pet or companion dog, it's not perfect—not quite.

Maynard, adult Tibetan Mastiff

24. The Tibetan Mastiff

If all the tales told about this breed are to be believed, it is the granddaddy of many of today's most popular dogs: New-foundlands, St. Bernards, Great Pyrenees, Mastiffs, Rott-weilers, and Great Danes. It is also the ancestor of that impressive group of ancient Roman war and guard dogs known as the Mollusers.

It is said that when he reached the farthest point east in his conquests, Alexander the Great was given several Tibetan Mastiffs to help him in his battles with elephants and lions.

These dogs were known to Genghis Khan and Attila the

Hun. When Marco Polo made his journey through the Orient in the thirteenth century he wrote about guard dogs the size of donkeys. These dogs are now believed to have been Tibetan Mastiffs. Later Western travelers in the mountains of Tibet and Bhutan spoke of the enormous dogs that people used to guard their herds of yaks. No one, save the owners, would dare approach these terrifying beasts.

A French traveler in Tibet in about 1800 met a group of nomadic herdsmen. The Nomads had a herd of three hundred yaks. At night the entire herd was guarded only by two gigantic Tibetan Mastiffs. He was so impressed by the size, power, and courage of these animals that he wrote in his journal that they would have been able to battle lions.

Today Tibet is ruled by China. During the 1960s in China all dogs, including the Tibetan Mastiff, were regarded as unnecessary. Many Chinese breeds became extinct, or nearly so. Fortunately for the Tibetan Mastiff, however, many examples of the breed had already reached the West, and its continued existence was assured.

Tibetan Mastiffs came to the West in many different ways, some honorably, some not so honorably. For example, the Dalai Lama, spiritual leader of Tibet, presented a pair of these rare dogs to President Dwight Eisenhower. One of the pups from this pair was given to Lowell Thomas, a well-known radio broadcaster and writer who had traveled in and written extensively on Tibet and had long been fascinated by rare dogs.

Then there were the less honorable ways. Smugglers would hide banned materials, including drugs, in false-bottomed crates containing Tibetan Mastiffs. Customs officials were often unwilling to look too closely at a crate containing so large and fierce an animal.

Some of these dogs ultimately came into the hands of

dog lovers and breeders who appreciated the qualities of the breed. Today, the Tibetan Mastiff, while certainly not common, is well established in the United States and elsewhere in the West, and its popularity is on the rise.

Tibetan Mastiff breeders believe that their dog is one of the most "natural" in existence. The owners of the Drakyi Tibetan Mastiff Kennels write: "Over the centuries, the dogs bred true in isolated areas of the Himalayas, and through the survival of the fittest, natural selection insured that the strongest and most genetically sound animals would survive to reproduce their own kind, making them quite distinct from the man-made breeds of today."

With most domestic dogs, the female comes into season twice a year. With the Tibetan Mastiff, the female comes into season only once a year, usually in the late fall or early winter. That is so that the pups will be born in the spring, and not have to undergo the rigors of the Tibetan winter until they are stronger and have a better chance of survival.

The Tibetan Mastiff comes in a huge variety of colors from solid black to bright tan and gold. They have a very harsh and durable coat, and a thick wooly undercoat. The animal's coat is so thick that they are hard to bathe, but they don't require any special clipping or other coat care. For these dogs of the Himalayas, the natural look is best.

But for all its "natural" and "primitive" qualities, and despite the reputation for ferocity, the Tibetan Mastiff is adapting remarkably well to modern civilized life. They are certainly not lap dogs—they are very large, the males measuring at least twenty-five inches at the shoulder. They have been known to weigh over 200 pounds, though that is not common.

As with any large breed, Tibetan Mastiffs require obedience training and strong control, and they tend to be fairly stubborn. They also need to be socialized, that is, introduced to people and other animals regularly from a young age. Yet the Tibetan Mastiff is not an overly aggressive dog. It was bred to protect, not to attack and fight. Modern breeders

Khamba, Tibetan Mastiff puppy

have tried to enhance the protective, not the attack, quality of the dog. If challenged on his own territory, a Tibetan Mastiff will not back down. They also bark fiercely, and the sight and sound of such a dog is likely to discourage all but the most determined intruder. They bark most frequently at night—something to think about if you have nearby neighbors.

A Tibetan Mastiff needs exercise because it is a large and active dog. A good-sized fenced yard and a long walk or two a day are necessities. While in the house the Tibetan Mastiff is usually quiet and well behaved.

All in all, this ancient breed seems to have a bright future.

Marguarita, a female Xolo, enjoying the sun

25. The Xoloitzcuintli

The dog's name is pronounced zo-low-eats-queen-tlee, but that's such a mouthful they're mostly just called Xolos (pronounced zo-lows.) You may have heard Xolos called by their other more familiar name, the Mexican Hairless. The breed comes in two sizes: Standard and Toy.

Clay figures of Xolos dating back as far as 1500 B.C. have been discovered and archaeologists have unearthed hundreds of ceramic images of these dogs at ancient Indian burial sites in Mexico. When the Spanish conquered Mexico in the sixteenth century, they wrote about the unusual hairless dogs the Aztec Indians kept as pets.

The dogs were believed to have magical healing powers and in remote parts of Mexico even today you'll find people who think that clutching a Xolo will cure colds, flu, whatever. The reason for this belief is probably the intense warmth of the Xolo's skin. When you're sick warmth feels good, so holding onto a Xolo might really make a person who is ill feel more comfortable.

Xolos aren't found only in ancient works of art but in modern ones, too. You'll see them in the murals (wall paintings) of the great Mexican painter Diego Rivera and the murals of the noted architect and artist Juan O'Gorman.

Despite their ancient lineage and popularity with artists, Xolos were on their way out in Mexico until they were rescued by the Mexican Kennel Club. The rescue effort began in the 1950s and today you'll find plenty of Xolos south of the border. Most live in Mexico City, Mazatlán, and Durango, on Mexico's west coast.

As for dog shows, it was in 1967 that the Xolo made its dramatic debut appearance on the international dog scene. That year a truly dazzling example of the Standard-sized variety of the breed was trotted around the European dog show circuit. Not only was the dog a huge crowd pleaser, it was the first Mexican dog in history to win an International Championship. After that great solo Xolo performance, the breed was on its way.

The Standard Xolo is an elegant canine which stands about twenty inches at the shoulder. It doesn't in the least look like the other famous Mexican dog, the Chihuahua. Despite the hairlessness in appearance, the Standard Xolo looks most like a small Doberman. Not necessarily 100 percent hairless, it may have wisps of short hair on its forehead and neck and may have some hair on its feet and near the end of its tail. It comes in a wide variety of colors like charcoal, slate, dark reddish-gray, liver, or bronze. The wisps of hair on black dogs are often red, which adds flair to their appearance. Though a dark solid body color is preferred, it's okay for the dog to have pink or coffee color spots on its skin.

In personality Standard Xolos are calm and cheerful. They don't attract fleas. They don't shed. They have no doggy odor. People allergic to furry dogs can sometimes fare well with the Xolo.

The Toy version has a lot in common with the Standard, but it is broad in the chest and ribs and except for a little fuzz or tufts of hair on the top of the head and the occasional few hairs on the tail, it is strikingly hairless. When most people think of a Mexican Hairless it's usually the Toy type of Xolo that comes to mind. Toy Xolos have super personalities. Friendly little animals, they love to curl up in their owner's lap. And they make excellent little watchdogs.

Additional Reading

Books

There are two books published in America concerned only with rare breeds:

Flamholtz, Cathy J. *A Celebration of Rare Breeds.* Fort Payne, Alabama: OTR Publications, 1986.

Gannon, Dee. *The Rare Breed Handbook.* Fairlawn, New Jersey: Golden Box Press, 1987.

There are many books which deal exclusively or primarily with breeds of dogs recognized by the American Kennel Club. Two of the best are:

The Complete Dog Book: The Official Publication of the American Kennel Club. New York: Howell Book House, Inc., updated regularly.

Caras, Roger (ed.). *Harper's Illustrated Handbook of Dogs.* New York: Harper & Row, 1985.

Magazines

The following all have information on both rare breeds and recognized breeds:

Dog Fancy. P.O. Box 6050, Mission Viejo, California 92690

Dog World. 29 N. Wacker Drive, Chicago, Illinois 60606

Kennel Review. 11331 Ventura Boulevard, Suite 301, Studio City, California 91604

This magazine is an official publication of the American Kennel Club and has information only on recognized breeds:

Pure-Bred Dogs/American Kennel Gazette, 51 Madison Avenue, New York, N. Y. 10010

Rare Breed Organizations

If you want more information about a particular breed write to:

Akbash Dog
Akbash Dog Association of America
P. O. Box 15238
Chevy Chase, Maryland 20815

American Hairless Terrier
c/o Edwin and Willie Scott
P. O. Box 79
Trout, Louisiana 71371

Argentine Dogo
International Argentine Dogo Club
c/o Cathy J. Flamholtz
Rt. 1, Box 180-A
Collinsville, Alabama 35961

Bolognese
Bolognese Club of America
P. O. Box 1461
Montrose, Colorado 81401

Canaan Dog
Canaan Club of America
c/o Lorraine Stephens
P. O. Box 55
Newcastle, Oklahoma 73065

Catahoula Leopard Dog
The National Association of Louisiana Catahoulas, Inc. (NALC)
P. O. Box 1041
Denham Springs, Louisiana 70727–1041

Cavalier King Charles Spaniel
Cavalier King Charles Spaniel Club, USA
c/o Mr. and Mrs. Gerald L. White
RFD 1, Box 21X
Strasburg, Virginia 22657

Chinese Crested
The American Chinese Crested Club
c/o Shirley C. Merrill, Registrar
3726 Eastman Road
Randallstown, Maryland 21133

Coonhounds
United Kennel Club (UKC)
100 East Kilgore Road
Kalamazoo, Michigan 49001–5596

Dogue de Bordeaux
c/o Peter Curley
S 8194 Hwy 78
Merrimac, Wisconsin 53561

Fila Brasileiro
Fila Brasileiro Club of America
P. O. Box 649
Manchester, Georgia 31816

Greater Swiss Mountain Dog
Greater Swiss Mountain Dog Club of America
c/o Dorothy M. Brackney
7218 Chatlake Drive
Dayton, Ohio 45424

Havanese
The Havanese Club of America
c/o Dorothy Goodale
P. O. Box 1461
Montrose, Colorado 81401

Jack Russell Terrier
The Jack Russell Terrier Breeders Association of America
P. O. Box 2326
Conway, New Hampshire 03818

Little Lion Dog
The Little Lion Dog Club of America
c/o Robert A. Yhlen
31 Byram Bay Road
Hopatcong, New Jersey 07843

Neapolitan Mastiff
The Neapolitan Mastiff Club of America
P. O. Box 40
Raritan, New Jersey 08869

Nova Scotia Duck Tolling Retriever
The Nova Scotia Duck Tolling Retriever Club, USA
c/o Marile Waterstraat
63 Blue Ridge Road
Penfield, New York 14526

Peruvian Inca Orchid
The Peruvian Inca Orchid Club of America
c/o Ginette Perez
P. O. Box 538
Westbrookville, New York 12785

Petit Basset Griffon Vendeen
The Petit Basset Griffon Vendeen Fanciers
c/o Barbara and Jeffrey Pepper
589 Oscawana Lake Road
Putnam Valley, New York 10579

PONS (Polish Lowland Sheepdog)
c/o Kazmir and Betty Augustowski
Elzbieta Kennels
1115 Delmont Road
Severn, Maryland 21144

Puffin Dog
The Norwegian Puffin Dog Club of America
c/o Paul Ross
Box 239
Conway, New Hampshire 03818

Shar-Pei
The Chinese Shar-Pei Club of America
55 Oat Court
Danville, California 94526

Shiba
The National Shiba Club of America
6912 Magnolia Avenue
Baltimore, Maryland 21227

Tibetan Mastiff
c/o Richard Eichorn
1145 Katey Lane
Simi Valley, California 93063

Xoloitzcuintli
The Xoloitzcuintli Club of America
c/o Ginette Perez
P. O. Box 538
Westbrookville, New York 12785

Photographic Credits

Index

United Kennel Club (UKC), 40, 42, 43

Val (Nova Scotia Duck Tolling Retriever), 79
Vladek (Polish Lowland Sheepdog), 90

Walker, John W., 39, 43
Walker, Thomas, 43
Washington, George, 39, 43, 46
Westminster Dog Show (New York), 35

White River King (Treeing Walker Coonhound), 45
Wirehaired Fox Terrier, 66
Wolfhound, Irish, 13

Xolo. *See* Xoloitzcuintli
Xoloitzcuintli, 1–2, 113–115

Yhlen, Bob, 71, 72
Yhlen, Carole, 71, 72

Zuber, June, 50

Susan and Daniel Cohen have authored a number of books for young readers, ranging from teenage social problems to teenage pop culture. Titles include *What You Can Believe About Drugs: An Honest and Unhysterical Guide for Teens, Rock Video Superstars,* and *A Six-pack and a Fake I.D.: Teens Look at the Drinking Question.*

Their interest in rare breeds of dogs goes back many years. One of the largest rare breed dog shows in the country is held not far from their home in Port Jervis, New York. They own a Clumber Spaniel, a rare but recognized breed and one of the biggest spaniels you will ever see. There are only about five hundred of them in the United States.